SINGLE DAD

RIVER LAURENT

ACKNOWLEDGMENTS

A big, big thank you to...

Leanore Elliott & Brittany Urbaniak & Peggy Schnurr

ISBN: 978-1-911608-15-8

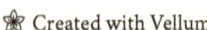 Created with Vellum

LINCOLN

"For the love of God, tell me something I don't already know!" I rage, slamming my open palms down on the conference room table. The water glasses tremble almost as hard as my management team. I don't care that I'm scaring the shit out of them. They deserve a lot fucking worse.

"We're going back through the logs right now." Ryland holds up his phone.

I see messages pouring in as the tech staff scramble to find the rat in our organization. "Yeah, too little, too late," I mutter. That sick, sweaty feeling is starting to work its paralyzing poison into every cell in my body. In two weeks, we're supposed to showcase our latest innovation in drone technology. Everything is ready, the press, the industry experts, the buyers, the government agencies, but my arch rival, Vince fucking Weissman stole our design and passed it off as his brainchild last night.

I loosen my tie. Hell, I can't even think straight. I take a deep breath and try to calm myself. This must be how people react when they find out all their years of slaving away have come to nothing. Jesus, everything we've worked for in the last three years—gone.

Millions of dollars' worth of research—flushed down the toilet.

My stomach twists with raw hate when I remember Weissman's smug smile, as he passed me in the hotel lobby last night. I was dying to wipe that grin off his arrogant face, but there was not a thing I could do to him. I had to nod politely, as if I wouldn't love to see him burn in hell, and move on.

"I'm sure they'll find something," Ryland soothes.

My head jerks up and I glare at him. "I hire the most talented people I can find, make them jump through about as many security hoops as candidates for the CIA do, get them to sign watertight contracts, and all for what?"

"Look, as soon as we know who stole the plans—"

"We already know who stole them," I snarl, and pushing myself out of my chair, I start walking away. There's a real danger I might launch myself across the table and strangle him. He's my best friend and we go a long way back, but fuck him for being so calm and reasonable while my whole life is falling apart.

I stare out of the window.

The bleak, rainy skyline is depressing, but even if the day were bright and sunny and full of unicorns sliding down fucking rainbows, it wouldn't help one bit. It's a waking nightmare. Behind me, the silence is so perfect you can hear a pin drop.

I turn around my eyes focusing on Laura Greenwell, the leader of my legal team. "Can we sue this fucker?"

She wants to say yes. She really does. I can tell by the way she presses her lips together and drums her fingernails restlessly on the table. "Weissman makes my blood boil, his methods have always been as unethical as sin—"

"Unethical? He outright stole our design!" I roar, barely able to hear myself think over the raging fury going on in my head.

She nods. "Yes. Yes, he did. He outright stole your design, but from a strictly legal standpoint, the patent on your drone is still pending, so Weissman Technologies had just as much right as anybody else to launch a demo last night. I'm sorry. I wish I could tell you something different, but we have no grounds to take him to court."

Lou's my chief of security who has been ominously quiet up to this point—probably because he is wondering if the leak occurred on his watch— speaks up for the first time, "What about an injunction?"

Laura shakes her head regretfully. "I mean, we could." She looks at me. "That's your call, naturally, but it will take weeks and—"

"—we have no way to prove that he stole it," I finish with an ever-sinking feeling in the pit of my stomach. "It'll be our word against theirs as to who stole the plans from whom. Scandal, mudslinging. Either we stand up for ourselves and look like a bunch of crybaby thieves, or we roll over like whipped dogs and let them pick up every damned contract that is rightfully ours to score."

"So what do we do now, boss?" Mark, my sales manager asks.

They're looking at me for the answers because I am the boss, the guy who's supposed to come up with the solutions. I turn away from them and stare unseeing out of the window. As a kid, my mother told me a story she read in the Reader's Digest. It was about this young woman who had spent all day cooking a turkey. A man she wanted to impress was coming to dinner. They had drinks, canapes and everything was going really well. Finally, it was time for the main course, the piece de résistance, the thing the young woman had worked on all day long.

Proudly, she carried in the perfectly done bird on a large tray. There were gasps of admiration from the assembled guests. As she crossed the threshold though, her shoe caught on the carpet. The tray jerked out of her hands. The turkey went flying across the room and landed on the floor.

There was a shocked silence in the room.

For a few shocked seconds nobody moved. The young woman was ready burst into tears. She couldn't believe her luck. All her hard work slaving in the hot kitchen had come to nothing. Then the girl's mother spoke up, "It's okay, darling. Throw this turkey away and serve the other one you roasted."

I turn around and look decisively at my management team, making sure to meet each member's eyes for emphasis. "We won't cancel the upcoming demo. We'll show them the other drone."

Ryland frowns. "What other drone?"

"The one Sam and her team are working on."

His jaw drops. "What are you talking about, Lincoln? That drone is months away from ready. It's has a major kink, remember? It can't pass the seven minutes mark without frying up its circuits. It'll never be ready in two weeks."

"Yes, it fucking will. It will, if I have to work twenty-four-seven myself," I growl.

"What about the rat?" Lou asks. "If we don't pin down exactly who took the plans and handed them over to the enemy, even the design for the second drone are in danger of falling into Weissman's hands.

"Oh, don't you worry. We'll find them, and I'll deal with them personally," I say softly.

"Mr. Cage?" Erica's voice rings through the room, via the speaker on the phone in the center of the table.

"What?" I demand, yanking the receiver from the base to keep the conversation between the two of us.

"I'm sorry, sir, but—"

"Which part of do not disturb me under any circumstances did you not understand?" I snap with irritation.

"I know, sir, but..." Her voice drops to a whisper. "Your...ex-wife is here."

LINCOLN

She might as well have thrown a bucket of ice water over me. I freeze in place, my mind the only thing still able to move. And it's racing. What the hell is she doing here? Is it Maddie? A shudder passes through me. Oh God, it must be Maddie. Suddenly, all the anger I felt about Weissman Technologies stealing my company's secrets disappears and I am filled with fear. Terrible, mouth drying, bone shriveling fear.

"Right, I'll come there," I say. Even my voice sounds strained and strange.

"Umm...sorry Mr. Cage, but she went straight into your office. I couldn't stop her. She's in there now."

"That's fine," I say automatically.

Ryland picks up on the change in my demeanor instantly and tries to catch my attention, but I avoid his gaze as I cross the room. This is the day from hell. *God, please let it not be about Maddie.* I open the door that connects the conference room to my office. My fists are clenched hard as I step through.

Fuck me.

The mind-numbing fear for Maddie drains from me in a rush, leaving me almost weak with relief. I close the door to give us a measure of privacy and lean back against it and survey the scene before me. My leather chair is tipped right back. Inside it is my ex-wife. There is a slight pout on her scarlet mouth, and her stiletto shod feet are resting on my desk. Against the leather and dark wood, she makes a languid, sensuous picture. For one second, a memory comes back. Those pale, smooth legs wrapped around my neck as I pound into her. Then the memory is gone, as quickly as it came, and I feel my balls shrink with revulsion.

Shit.

I need to get laid.

Badly.

Now that I know nothing is wrong with Maddie, I have no time for whatever it is she is up to. I need to get rid of her, and fast. I glance at my watch. "What's this all about, Regina? I don't have the time today."

She sniffs derisively. "There's something new. Lincoln, not having the time."

I frown. "I'm serious. What do you want? And can you fucking get out of my chair?"

Setting her feet on the ground in a smooth movement, she stands. As always, she makes a stunning picture. She is the mistress of the little black dress. Nobody wears it better than her. Still a little dressed up for lunch with the girls. Then again, it's been a very long time since I cared enough to keep tabs on her schedule. My eyes rove over her. I have to admit

7

I'm impressed by the amount of money she's wearing around her neck and ears. I've bought enough jewelry in my lifetime to know the good stuff when I see it. She must have found a new sucker to buy them for her.

I sit behind the desk. The chair is still warm from her body. "Well?" I prompt, impatiently.

She goes to stand at the other side of the desk. "I thought you should know that I've decided to let you spend a little time with Madison."

Not many things in this wide, wide world can surprise me. I admit, the news that Weissman poached our technology stunned me this morning, but that's probably naiveté on my part. This is a cutthroat business and he is known in the business for questionable ethics. But this? If she set the soles of my shoes on fire right this minute, it wouldn't surprise me more than what she just announced.

"You've decided to let me spend a little time with Madison?" I repeat. I have to be sure I actually heard right. With the way things have gone today, I could be hearing things.

She lifts one shoulder. "Yes, I thought it would be nice for her to spend the summer with you."

Whoa! Pigs do fly. I open my mouth in amazement. "The summer with me?"

"Are you going to repeat everything I say?" she asks sarcastically.

I feel anger boil up in my body. She really picked the wrong day to have this conversation with me. "What do you expect? For the last two years, you have behaved as if any time

Madison spends with me could actually be detrimental to her mental and physical health."

"If you had been a better father…" She lets her voice trail off.

"Fuck you, Regina. You know, I was the best father in the world to that little girl while we were together. We could've arranged joint custody, if you weren't such a selfish bitch, but after dragging me through the court system for a solid year, fighting me tooth and nail and going for sole custody of our daughter, you now stroll in here and talk about handing her over to me for the summer?" I lean back and remember how bad it'd been. "Oh yeah, and what happened to I'm such a lousy father I'll neglect my child and cause her to suffer mental abuse equivalent to solitary confinement?" I sneer.

"Well…" She shrugs. "People change. It looks like you've matured now. I should give you a chance. Besides, she was very young then and she needed more supervision. She's quite the grown-up now. You'll be able to handle her no problem."

My eyes widen. "Jesus Christ, Regina. You're passing her on to me because you've grown tired of her, haven't you?" And that's it. I can tell my assessment has hit a little too close to home by the way she lifts her chin defiantly.

"Don't be horrible," she whines. "You know how much I love Madison."

What the hell did I ever see in this woman? "Actually, it doesn't look like you love Madison very much from where I'm sitting. It looks like playing Mommy is no fun anymore now that you can't use it to hurt me," I observe.

She sniffs and straightens her spine. "It doesn't matter what it looks like to you. She needs her father, Lincoln. That's the reality here."

I jump to my feet, palms on the desk, leaning across the surface to bridge some of the distance between us. Her expensive perfume wraps itself around my head in a cloud. "You can't just walk into my office and demand I take our child when the court ruled in your favor two years ago. Have you even stopped to think how this will upend her life? She's six years old, Regina. She needs structure and routine, not to be bounced around from you to me, and back to you again, just because you're bored."

"Maybe she doesn't have to come back to me, then," she fires back.

I rear back in shock. My jaw might even have dropped. I stare at her and she stares back. So this is what she really wants, and she wants it badly too. My poor little girl.

She lifts her chin. "I'm going back to Europe tomorrow with the new man in my life. So, there's little room for argument now. She's all yours."

My head spins. What? Tomorrow? She's dumping our daughter at my door and leaving the country tomorrow. There's no more patience left in me. I used it up hours ago. "How dare you?" I shout, raising my voice with every word. "How can you expect me to drop everything like this, when I have no arrangements in place for her?"

"That's what nannies are for," she reminds me in an icy tone. She opens her purse and takes out a pair of sunglasses.

I watch in amazement as she slides them onto her face.

Her full mouth purses in a studied pout. "Nobody's asking

you to give up your life, Lincoln. Or your precious business. Just be a father. You've done it before. It's like riding a bicycle. You'll be fine."

I shake my head. This is it. I'm actually about to lose my mind. I'm about to go over the edge. "You think I can find a goddamned nanny by tomorrow?" I shout.

"You might want to keep your voice down," she says with sugary sweetness. "You don't want to teach her any foul language, do you?"

As though I haven't heard her swear like a drunken sailor. Before I can remind her to keep her opinions of my choice of language to herself, her message filters through. "Wait a minute. Maddie is here?"

There's that practiced one-shouldered shrug again. "Yeah. She's outside. Didn't Erica tell you?"

No. She fucking did not. I stare at her in disbelief.

"Look, if it makes you feel any better, I've got this for you." She opens her purse and pulls out a thick envelope. Then she holds it out to me.

I don't take it. I don't even dare to think it could be what I hope, pray it could be. Of course, it's not. After all, this is the day from hell.

"It's the custody papers. I've signed Madison over to you. Just suck it up and do your duty. You are her father, after all."

My eyes nearly drop out of my head. My mouth falls open too, but I quickly snap it shut and frown. It takes a lot to leave me speechless, but that's where I am right now.

My cunning ex-wife recognizes this. She trains her cornflower blue eyes on me and flutters her lashes. She knows her eyes are her greatest asset. Once they used to set my pulse racing. Now, they leave me stone-cold.

Maybe they always left me cold.

Maybe, I should've been honest with myself in those days before the wedding, when I let the fact that I was a kid from Bay Ridge and I was marrying a Park Avenue princess blind me. Sure, Regina seemed perfect on paper: beautiful, educated, connected, wealthy, and the sex was always hot, but she wasn't warm or real. There was never anything behind those icy eyes.

She comes from a family with ice water running in their veins.

As a matter of fact, I can't remember ever seeing either of my ex-in-laws hug or kiss their daughter. Not even on our wedding day. They were a breed of people different from me. If one single word could sum up my childhood, it was "warmth." A life full of hugs, praise and appreciation. I knew even then that our marriage was doomed, but I built her up in my head. I wanted it to work. She was like that Rolls Royce you dream of having.

I take the envelope from her hand. Part of me still thinks this is a trick. Is she really giving Madison back to me?

"It's a shame we broke up," she murmurs. "I've yet to meet a guy with a bigger or angrier dick than yours. Sometimes, I still miss it."

"Get out, Regina," I mutter from between clenched teeth.

She grins. She always had skin thicker than a rhino's hide. "Okay, okay. Don't bite my head off. I'm going."

I watch her turn on her heels and walk away.

She turns at the door. "Oh, one more thing. Maddie has chicken pox. It's just the remnants of the disease, but she doesn't looks so good."

"What?" I bellow. "You dragged her halfway around the world while she is sick?"

"Don't be so dramatic. We flew first class, obviously. She's fine."

I can't believe this. I knew Regina was a nasty, callous, heartless monster, but I've never seen anything like this. The selfishness it takes to do something like this. What kind of mother would drag her sick daughter out this way, when she ought to be in bed? Her own bed, in her own room.

The door shuts. I stare at it. Still in disbelief. Fuck. Maddie had chicken pox and I didn't even know about it. I *am* a lousy father. I raise my hand and look at the document. I'm clutching it so hard—I'm nearly crushing it. I relax my hand. I take the document out and look at my ex-wife's signature.

Hell, she actually did it.

She gave me custody!

Suddenly, Weissman and the leak in my company feel like they are nothing. I got my daughter back. I look out of the window and a ray of sunshine is trying to burst from behind a dark cloud.

I couldn't afford to show Regina how happy I felt when she stood here in my office. I know what she is like. Vindictive. A dog in the manger. Even if she doesn't want something, she can't bear for anyone else to have it. It would kill her to know she just gave me the thing I want most in life. She could have so easily withdrawn her offer. But she didn't. I have the paperwork in my hands.

Maddie is mine, mine, mine!

I punch the air and a whoop of pure joy escapes my mouth. I stride over to the door, open it a crack, and listen.

"I love you, my darling," Regina is saying.

"I love you too, Mommy," Maddie replies dutifully.

"Be a good girl for mommy, okay?"

"I will."

"Goodbye darling. I'll call you when I get to France."

"All right. Goodbye, Mommy." Her voice is forlorn and small.

It hurts me a little. Poor thing is going to be ripped away from everything she knows. But I can give her better life. I know I can.

I wait until the sound of Regina's stilettos start to die away, then I open the door and my heart breaks.

LINCOLN

Oh, Maddie.

Too sick to care very much where she is, or what is happening around her, she is sitting huddled up in one corner of the big, black leather sofa in Erica's office. Her head is turned to watch the departing figure of her mother, but her mittened hands scratch restlessly at her itchy skin.

Mittens?

One of Regina's pathetic attempts at mothering her child.

Poor mite. To think Regina flew her across the Atlantic while she is in this condition. She looks so small and vulnerable.

She turns her face back, and sees me. The light from the iPad on her lap shines on her little face, highlighting how many angry red marks there are on her skin. "Daddy," she whispers.

I know that voice. It comes out when she is very tired, or sick. I walk up to her, push the two pieces of Louis Vuitton luggage on the floor away, and crouch down in front of her.

Her eyes are red and crusty. The last thing she should be staring at is her iPad. Gently, I take it from her lap and put it on the sofa out of her reach. I touch her forehead. She doesn't seem to have a temperature. "Hey," I say softly.

She blinks hard and tries not to cry. Her mouth trembles and she presses her lips together to take back some control. "Do you think I'll ever see Mommy again?"

I frown with surprise. "Of course, you will."

She sniffs. "Are you sure?"

"What makes you think you won't?" I ask curiously.

"Because," she pauses to wipe her nose. "I know Juan doesn't like me. He told Mommy he wants her to have his child. Then it would be just theirs."

"Oh, honey," I whisper, and wrap her small body in my arms. I want to fucking kill Regina and her stupid boyfriend. "Your mommy is always going to your mommy, okay? Nobody and nothing can change that, do you hear me? Your mommy needs to go to Europe for a bit so I asked her if I could take care of you and she said yes."

She moves and stares at me with big eyes. "You did?"

"Of course."

"But Mommy said, you didn't want me because you were too busy in the office."

Jesus Christ, I swear I could cheerfully wring Regina's neck. "I think Mommy might have misunderstood. I've never said that. I always wanted you to live with me, but until recently, you were too young to come and stay with me so the Judge decided that you should stay with Mommy until you were old enough. Now that you are old enough and Mommy is going to be busy in Europe for a few months, we decided that you should come stay with me. If things work out and you like living here, then you can even stay here with me. Is that okay with you?"

She smiles shyly then nods.

"Good. The thing is, I'm not really prepared. Mommy and I were thinking that you would be coming in a couple of weeks, but as it turns out you've arrived early and while that makes me super happy, I am not really prepared. I have an emergency at the office and I don't have the apartment ready for you yet, so will you forgive Daddy if everything is not exactly the way it should be for the next few days?"

She stares at me. "What do you have to do to prepare, Daddy?'

"Well, loads of things. I mean, your room is not even painted yet." I grin at her. "Which, maybe that is a good thing, because now you get to pick out your own favorite color."

She smiles, that impish smile that I haven't seen for ages. Come to think of it, every time I've spoken to her on Skype, Regina was always hovering in the background and Maddie always seemed a bit distracted and distant.

"Can I have more than one color, Daddy?"

I grin. "It's your room, so you can have as many colors as you want."

Her eyes grow as big as saucers. "Really?"

"Sure," I say with a shrug. "What colors were you thinking of?"

She starts ticking the colors off on her fingers. "Red, blue, yellow, purple, and green. Oh, and pink."

My eyes widen, then I chuckle at her excitement. "Oh, wow."

She nods solemnly. "I've got a unicorn and I want him to be comfortable in my room."

I nod. "Okay. The thing is I'm really, really busy for the next few days, so I won't be able to get your room organized that fast."

She claps her hands "I know what. I can camp out here with you. All I need is a tent."

I stare at her. My daughter never fails to amaze me. "You want to live in a tent in my office?"

Her eyes shine. "Can I?"

I rub my jaw. It would be a terrible, terrible thing to do and yet, it would be the fucking perfect solution until I can get a Nanny sorted out, and I can figure out how to solve my problems at work.

"Please say, yes, Daddy. Please. Please. Please?" she begs.

My parents would have had a heart attack. My staff will think I've gone mad. If Regina finds out, she might try to take back custody of Maddie back. I run my hands through my hair.

"Please, Daddy?"

Fuck it. So what if it isn't the norm? At least this way, I'll have her with me. I smile. "All right, just until I get a Nanny for you and do up your room, okay?"

"Yah, Yah, Yah," she sings happily.

Erica comes in. "Do you want me to get anything for you, or Madison, Mr. Cage?"

"Yeah. I need you to go get some stuff. We'll need blankets, pillows, lots of toys, one of those multicolored Princess tents." I look at my daughter. "Did I miss anything?"

"Ice cream," Maddie pipes up immediately.

I wink at her then turn back to Erica's dumbfounded expression, and add, "A small freezer for the ice cream and a lot of fluids, including milk."

"Okay. Anything else?"

"Yeah. Find out if everybody in the office has already had chicken pox."

LINCOLN

I t surprises me how independent Maddie is. The kid effortlessly amuses herself for hours while I meet with my tech team. There's just no way around it. My company is going to the wall and damn me, if I don't do everything in my power to avert that.

We have dinner together, which is quite frankly, the highlight of my day from hell, but every time my phone rings, and I have to take the call, she just quietly continues with her meal while I'm on the phone. I don't know whether to be impressed, or saddened by her maturity. When we get back to the office, I offer to read her a bedtime story.

"Daddy, I *can* read, you know," she explains with world-weary patience.

"I know you can, but sometimes, it's really nice when someone else reads for you."

She thinks about it. "Okay," she says, grinning up at me.

I smile back at her, but it troubles me that she has missed out on so much. How could I have been so caught up with work that I know almost nothing about her upbringing? I'm going to have to buy more clothes for her too. Her suitcase is full of designer party dresses. Not a single pair of jeans in sight. It's enough to make me wonder what my daughter's life has been like for the last two years.

You could've found out for yourself.

The nagging, knowing voice in the back of my head isn't going to lie down and let me get away with anything today. It is true I could've pushed to be a bigger part of her life. Even if I didn't have shared custody—a blow that took a long time to get over—I should've pressed for more visitation. A few times a year, plus a little time around her birthday and the holidays wasn't nearly enough.

Obviously, since I know so little about her life.

We go back to my office that now looks like a giant play-room. Erica found a pink princess castle tent with turrets. She also bought a blow-up dragon, and a whole load of toys and books.

Maddie changes into her pajamas and brushes her teeth in my bathroom. She asks me to plait her hair for her.

"Why?" I ask.

"Because it will be a horrendous mess when I wake up and Mommy says I have to have my hair in braids. Christina always makes two braids."

"Right," I say taking the brush from her hand. I try very hard, but braiding hair is more complicated than it seems at first.

"Are you finished, Daddy?" she asks for the tenth time.

"Never mind. We'll deal with the mess in the morning," I say, swallowing my frustration. I will have to get someone to teach me. "Come on. Let's get you to bed. What story do you want?"

"Can we read The Little Mermaid please?" she asks politely, as she settles into the sweet smelling, freshly laundered blankets.

I'll have to remember to give Erica a bonus this month. She went out of her way to make sure that my sick little girl has everything she could possibly need. "Of course." I climb into the tent and using a flashlight, I read her book to her.

Poor child, she is so exhausted she falls asleep halfway through the book.

Gently, I kiss her spotty cheek and holding my breath, I carefully slide out of her tent.

I stand and look down at her. Something tugs at my heart. My child is asleep on my office floor, instead of in a bedroom in my apartment. That's where she should be, permanently. And will be. As soon as I sort out my business. She deserves better than this, damn it.

I have to get my mind back on work. Two weeks. Two weeks until the conference launch. The thought of it makes me feel sick. Though, that could be the stress. Or just plain ole seething rage. It consumes me every time I remember Weissman's arrogant, taunting smile as he passed me by last night.

I run my hands through my hair as the adrenaline in my blood spikes. I can't let it take over again. I'll end up collapsing and my business—not to mention the little girl in the next room—need me badly. He thinks he's got me. Well, he hasn't. I gear myself up for a long, long night. What I need is an energy drink. I tiptoe out of my office to get one of the cans Erica stocks the fridge with.

My hand lingers on the doorknob as I turn back to look at the tent. I'm only going to be seconds. But what if she wakes up and finds herself in a strange place? She could go into panic mode and I wouldn't hear her. All the walls are sound-proof. With good reason. Before today, my ultimate priority in this place was confidentiality. A lot of good that did me. I leave the door open, grab a can, and go back into my office.

All is quiet in the tent.

I collapse into the chair behind my desk and realize I'm sitting on my suit jacket, but I can't bring myself to care. My eyes itch with fatigue and I don't think I've ever felt this drained. Not when I ran in that half-marathon at school, not when I was working overnight to put myself through college. Not even when Maddie was a newborn and she used to scream all night with colic and nothing worked, not gripe water, not anything, except being swaddled tightly in a blanket and bounced on my knees for hours. Every time I thought she'd finally fallen asleep and tried to put her down, the ear-piercing screaming would begin all over again.

Of course, Regina always claimed she suffered from post-partum depression and needed her sleep, so it was all up to me. For nearly five months, I did the night shift. Even then, when I would stumble into work with eyes that burned out from exhaustion and lack of sleep, I didn't feel nearly as wrung-out as I do now.

My head is killing me. No wonder I can't focus on anything. I throw a handful of the aspirin down my throat and take a gulp of my drink. That should help. I close my eyes and lean back for a few minutes. There is a quiet sigh from the tent and my eyes snap open.

She is sucking her thumb in her sleep.

I remember her unhappy little face this morning, when her mother abandoned her in my waiting room. How many times has she been passed around over the two years during the time she's been in her mother's care? How many people have actually truly cared for her?

Regina's high and mighty parents? No fucking way. They wouldn't know what care meant if it sat up and bit them in the ass. They hated me. Even though I'd already made a name for myself in the tech world by the time I married Regina, and they couldn't quite get away with accusing me of marrying their daughter for their money, they never stopped dropping sly hints.

Maddie's days of being passed around are over.

I'll hire a nanny, but I don't plan on palming my kid off on anybody else. She deserves a happy life. The sort of parent who would hang her artwork on the fridge and attend all of her little school shows. Do schools still do that? I wouldn't know. I've never attended anything, since Regina cut me off from all knowledge of my child's life.

Still not her fault. I could've pushed back, if I wasn't so fucking focused on my business. Well, I've got my priorities in order now.

I peer into the dim of the tent entrance. Her curly hair is like a brown cloud around her head. At least the itching has stopped now that she's asleep. She's like a little angel, so peaceful. My heart has never felt so full. She needs a father with his shit together. I have to be that father.

"I'm going to do my best for you," I whisper, still watching her sleep. "I just don't know what that looks like yet. I need to figure it out. So you might have to be a little patient with me while I get it together. I've been alone for a long time. I need to adjust."

I turn and catch my reflection in the glass windows. It's nearly ten o'clock and the glass is a mirror. There I am...a guy who looks like he's been dragged backwards through a thorn bush. I barely recognize myself. My hair is in complete disarray from running my hands through it all day, my shirt is rumpled from sliding around in the tent, and my collar is wide open. Only the devil knows where I left my tie.

I look away. I need to get my head on straight. Prioritize. Take advantage of the fact that Maddie is asleep and get some work done. I still have hours of work to do.

I sure as hell can't let the night escape me. I'm fighting for all I've worked for now. I open my emails and skim the subject lines, my eyes burning.

SAMANTHA

"Okay. This is it. This one's for all the marbles." I stop, cocking my head to the side. There's nobody around to hear me at this time of night. I'm talking to myself again. Very worrying.

With my pen poised over the clipboard, I hit the start button on the video camera, then the green square on the computer screen.

"Here goes. Attempt one thousand at running the drone without the battery overheating."

I watch the drone fly in circles two feet below the ceiling. The minutes tick away. Twenty-five seconds to go before we hit the threshold where the temperature has always spiked and fried the circuits.

"Come on, baby. Come on. You can do this. Just stay cool. Stay cool." I'm chewing my lip hard enough for it to hurt as my eyes keep darting back and forth from the hovering drone to the clock. The seventh minute mark hits and I hold my breath.

Please, please, please....

The first sizzle tells me it's over and my heart sinks as fast as the drone. It hits the metal table with a sickening sound. The familiar smell of burning fills the room.

"Son of a bitch!" I groan, slamming the clipboard down. Nervous energy makes me pace the floor like a caged animal before I drop into a chair and stare at the ceiling. I've tried every tweak I can think of.

I drop my head into my hands and closing my eyes, hold it for a minute. What am I supposed to do now? A sense of hopelessness settles over me. It's been weeks I've been trying to tackle this issue and I'm not any further ahead than I was on day one. To top it all, the big cheese has sent down a missive through Ryland, my immediate boss— the drone has to be ready to be shown to the public in two weeks!

The air in Ryland's office turned blue when he gave me that juicy bit of information.

"What am I missing?" I mutter, springing up and walking to the table where all the stats are spread out. Two weeks until we go to demo and I have no idea how to stop this drone from crashing and burning in less than seven minutes. I switch on the extractor fans and go back over the data from the last ten tests. There has to be something I'm missing. I bet it'll end up being the stupidest possible oversight, too. I must be overthinking it. I must be.

I roll my head on my neck to work out the kinks. My jaw hurts. I've been clenching my teeth for most of the day. That's what I do when I'm stressed out. I rub my fingertips along the hinge of my jaw. Is it called a hinge? I don't know. I don't know anything anymore, evidently. According to some people, I never have.

What would my Dad think if he saw me standing here, floundering, giving myself a jaw massage? That he was right. As always. The jerk. My jaw tightens again and I know I shouldn't think about him if I want to think straight.

Click.

I jump at the familiar, but unexpected, sound of the security locks behind me. Who else is here at nearly midnight? I thought I was the only crazy one. Must be Ryland. I turn around. Of course, it is. I'm glad he's here. If anybody will understand the frustration plaguing me, it's him.

"Ryland?" I say, dropping into the big leather chair behind the table. "You're still here?"

"You certainly are perceptive," he says dryly. Perching on the edge of my desk, he loosens the tie I can't believe he's still wearing at this time of night.

I lean back in the chair until I'm practically reclined and heave a sigh. "You really should talk to your boss about the hours he expects you to keep."

He shrugs. "Well, he expects it of himself too."

"Yeah? Well, I'm surprised. He's sort of a dick."

His wince tells me I've gone too far. "Now, now. Your personal problems with Lincoln are no concern of mine. We've discussed this before."

"I know, I know. I'm just tired and frustrated. I don't even know the guy. I guess arrogant bullies just rub me up the wrong way."

"That's right. You don't know him. He's not a bad guy. Sure, he's a slave driver, but look at what he's built with his bare hands." He leans forward with the cocky smile I've learned to like. "And he signs your paychecks."

"He does not. I get direct deposit."

"Same difference." His attention falls on the drone, still sitting where it crashed on the table. He scowls and looks at me sideways. "Still checking out at seven minutes, huh?"

"Afraid so," I mutter, and start massaging my jaw again, as stress threatens to overtake me.

"If there's anybody who can figure this out, I know it's you. I wouldn't have handed this project to you if I didn't have ultimate faith in you."

"You're doing it, you know."

"Doing what?"

I throw a withering look his way that he knows has absolutely no bite to it. "Telling me what you think I want to hear, so you can squeeze more and more work out of me. Bolstering my confidence, so I'll have the big breakthrough which reflects well on you."

He throws back his head and laughs, reminding me once again, why of the two of them, I prefer him over his best friend, and the Big Guy. Bossman. The one that everyone is soooooo in awe of. I have a few other names for him, but I know better than to let them fly in front of Ryland. How could two men practically grow up together but end up so vastly different?

"As much as it tickles me to think of your work reflecting

29

well on me, you would do well to remember that it's your position in the company which sort of hinges on this. That is to say, your upward mobility. Not to mention that lovely bonus waiting for you."

"Right now, I'd give anything just to make that damn drone upwardly mobile." The bonus is not important to me. If it were money I wanted, I could have just worked for my father. Or just looked for a rich husband like my stepsister.

"It's already upwardly mobile. The trick is making it stay that way." He walks over, picks it up, and turns it over in his large hands. Holding it, he faces me. "I know you can figure this out, Sam. I have faith in you. That's not smoke up your ass, either. I mean that."

"I know you do. I wonder if El Capitan will feel the same way when he finds out I'm still bombing."

"You have the chance to find out for yourself." He grins.

"What do you mean?"

"I mean, I came down here to tell you that he asked to see us."

"And you left him waiting all this time, while the two of us sat here talking?" I jump out of my chair like it's on fire.

"Whew," he teases. "For somebody who claims she doesn't like Lincoln, she sure hops up like she can't wait to see him."

That irritates me. "Shut up."

He grins. "I'm just saying."

"And I'm just saying you really need to start getting more sleep if you think you're being funny right now." Lincoln Cage is everything I hate about men, wrapped up in one tall, dark, smug, sexy package. Mr. Ultra-Masculine. God, I can't stand him.

If I were on Dr. Freud's couch, he'd have some pretty clear ideas on why I feel the way I do. He'd wrap me up with a neat little bow and call it daddy issues. Lincoln Cage is a younger, hotter version of my dad. Unfortunately, he also happens to be more brilliant than my stepfather. Much as I hate to, I have to respect his achievements. Ryland is right about all the incredible things Lincoln has done in the short time he's been in this industry.

"What does he want from us?" I ask as I try to match my stride to Ryland's looping long one out of the engineering department and down the hall to the elevator which will take us up to his office. I've never been up there. I've never ranked high enough.

"A report on our progress. We had a bit of an emergency meeting today and he wanted something from me by close of business, but I knew you'd be burning the midnight oil and wanted to wait until your latest tests were complete."

"Emergency meeting?"

"It's a long story." He waves it off. "Anyway, he'll want to know how this issue is progressing."

"What you're telling me is, I have to present a report to the CEO of the company, and I have roughly the next half-minute to prepare it."

"Something like that. Yes."

I have to lean against the wall of the elevator car for strength. "Great. Just so we're clear."

"Fair warning," he adds, glancing my way. "He's had a really, really bad day."

There are only two things keeping my mouth shut right now. First, the fact that Ryland went to bat for me when it came time to hire a young woman as his Senior Engineer. Without him, I wouldn't have a job in the first place. Second, the fact that he and Lincoln are so close, he's obviously going to feel sorry for his best friend.

So, instead of informing him that Lincoln Cage can stuff his bad day where the sun doesn't shine, I simply reply, "Oh. Well. I wonder how that feels."

"No smartass remarks."

"You don't have much faith in me, do you?" I eye him up and wonder just what he thinks of me.

"Oh, I have faith enough," he assures me with a grin. "But maybe because we're far too much alike. I see a lot of me in you so let me warn you, your quick-witted jabs won't be appreciated in this situation."

"I'll play nice," I promise, leaving out the part where Lincoln had better hope he plays nice, too. I've never been good at rolling over for a belly rub, no matter who I'm up against or how much leverage they have on me.

LINCOLN

Where the fuck is Ryland? I love the guy as much as I could ever love another man, but there are times when I worry that he takes a little too much for granted. Like the limits of my patience. He has saved my life in more ways than one. He keeps me from blowing up daily and God knows, my Engineering and Development department wouldn't be in half the shape they're in if it weren't for him. He knows talent when he sees it and he knows how to keep them performing using a slick carrot and stick method he has turned into an art.

But I don't take this slack shit lightly. I shouldn't have to wait so damned long for a face-to-face. He's kept me waiting exactly seventeen minutes. Sixteen minutes too long. The sound of leisurely footsteps outside the conference door sparks my outrage further. "What took you so long?" I look up from the monitor to glare at him.

He has the good sense to at least look cowed by my reaction as he pauses in the doorway. "Sorry," he replies, as he steps aside to reveal the petite, curvaceous, sapphire-eyed blonde behind him.

Oh, I get it now. He's been lounging around with our newest Senior Engineer, his protégé, Sam or whatever-her-name-is. He fooled me with that little nickname of hers, made me believe he was hiring a man. Not that there's anything wrong with women working in tech—I'm not a monster from the stone ages—but for some weird reason, she grates on my nerves.

One of those girls who think it's a good idea to wear shapeless, masculine clothes and call themselves by male names. My brain notes the way she has pulled her long, golden hair back in a tight ponytail. No makeup either, though she's young and pretty enough to not need it. Even so, couldn't she try to be slightly feminine? She's wearing loafers, for God's sake. Although, there isn't much she can do to hide what she has going on under that crisp shirt and slacks. If I wasn't so exhausted and put-out...My gaxe travel upwards to meet hers.

She lifts her chin and stares at me with those beautiful eyes, but in exactly the way a certain ex-wife of mine likes to do.

In fact, it's the way she stared at me earlier today. Just like that, all thoughts pertaining to her body and what is or isn't softly jiggling under her blouse—vanish. "Oh, I see. You're the one holding up the works, then?" I ask.

She blinks, as though she doesn't understand the question. "I'm sorry. I wasn't aware that we'd perfected teleportation yet." Then she shoots a look at a very flustered Ryland. "Was that done in-house?"

He grimaces, shrugging at me in an apologetic way. *Women. What can you do?*

I'd love to tell him right now what I'd like to do, but I don't feel like giving her room to bring me up on charges of unprofessionalism or whatever she might come up with. I narrow my eyes. "Miss…"

"Harper," she replies, all but rolling her eyes when I don't remember her last name.

I do remember it, but I would rather have her think that I don't. An age-old tactic. Make sure they know how unimportant they are. Keep them from getting too big a head about themselves. "Miss Harper, I don't know how Ryland conducts business down in your department, but I think it's only fair to inform you of my intolerance for backtalk. We're not friends. We're barely colleagues, and seeing as how you haven't held your position for very long, I'd be very careful about what you say."

"Fair enough," she murmurs. But she doesn't apologize.

I'm wise enough to know how to pick my battles and this isn't one worth fighting. She's just a stubborn little shit and she needs to be knocked down a peg or two. Or more. But I don't have the time or the inclination. "I didn't ask to see you both," I say to Ryland, as I pointedly ignore Samantha's gaze. She's looking around the place as though she's sizing it up for her own use one day. The audacity of this girl is unreal.

"I know, but Sam has been working on that bug I told you about…"

I can't help myself, I turn to Samantha. "Excuse me. Can I get you a tape measure, so you can take note of the room's dimensions for later use?"

A ghost of a smile flickers across her face. "No, no, I'm fairly good at eyeballing measurements." And damned if her blue eyes don't drift down to my crotch before bouncing back up to my face.

"As I was saying," Ryland continues, all but stepping between me and the girl to get my attention. "Sam has been working out that bug we talked about."

"Working it out?" I ask, intrigued. "Does that mean it's been fixed?"

He winces. "Bad choice of words, I guess."

"So it's not fixed?" I look at her, one eyebrow raised.

"I was working on it just now, before being interrupted."

"Nobody asked for you to be here." I look at Ryland again, sending a silent message. He needs to get this girl in line and fast, or I can't guarantee she'll have a job with the company by morning. I have enough problems on my mind right now. There are a million engineers out there with the skills this girl has. I'm still not certain I understand why he had such a hard-on for hiring her. Unless it was a literal hard-on, but she's not anywhere near his type. If anything, I'd expect him to end up with a woman like Regina.

"She knows more about the issue than I do, since she's been working on it exclusively ever since we discovered it." He turns to her with a scowl. "Tell him what you've found."

She takes a deep breath.

I don't miss the way her already generously endowed tits expand when she does. What the fuck is the matter with me?

Her voice is lower when she starts talking about her work, "I just ran another test, and there's been no improvement. At around six-and-a-half minutes, the battery burns too hot and fries everything."

"Son of a bitch." I want to sweep everything off my desk and maybe throw the huge, mahogany monstrosity out the window while I'm at it. "How many different types of battery did you use?"

"The lithiums are the only ones with enough juice to sustain the sort of long-range travel you're looking to support," she points out. "They just burn too hot after that amount of time. The design has the battery casing placed too close to the motherboard, to make things worse."

"So you're faulting the design," I mutter, my hackles up once again. The design is my baby, and she knows that.

"I didn't place fault anywhere. I'm merely stating a fact. You want to be kept abreast of how we're progressing. Well, that's the state of affairs."

"What about a higher-powered fan inside the casing?" Ryland suggests. "Anything to keep the temperature down."

"Tried it—anything stronger is naturally...larger." Her glance slips down to my crotch and color stains her neck and cheeks.

The first time she did do it in retaliation. She'd caught me checking out her boobs and it became an anything you can do, I do thing, but this time it was completely involuntary.

Suddenly, my cock takes over and thoughts pop into my head.

She's actually fucking gorgeous. I could do things with her. Bend her over the desk. Fuck her until she screams.

I should have cleaned myself up a little.

She probably thinks I'm a complete mess. Easily rattled, poorly groomed.

Then, thank God, my brain takes over again. Damn it all, what the fuck am I doing getting distracted by one of my staff? I'm fighting for my life here. I'm just tired and off guard. I resist the urge to roll up my sleeves and glare at her. She is the cause of my slip of judgement. There is no place for sex pots like her in these kinds of jobs.

"It would entail a total redesign, which we all know there isn't any time for," she finishes, looking at Ryland.

"Find a way to better insulate the circuitry, then," I bark.

She tilts her head to the side, eyes narrowed to slits. If looks could kill, I'd be six feet under.

SAMANTHA

Find a way to better insulate the circuitry. No freaking kidding. "Thank you so much for your sage, expert advice," I whisper through gritted teeth. There goes my jaw hinge again.

"Excuse me?" Lincoln holds up a palm in Ryland's face when he tries to step in. "You're damn right, it's expert advice. I'm the CEO of this company and I built it from the ground up, in case you've forgotten."

"I haven't forgotten."

"I would hope not, seeing as how you've been here for all of three minutes and therefore, would've only just found out about the company history. If you couldn't manage to retain that information, I'd have to question your abilities in other areas."

"Oh, my abilities are just fine," I snap. God, who does this jerkwad think he is? God's greatest gift? I can hardly stand the sight of the snide, domineering creep. No wonder he's divorced. Who could stand living with him? Another one of the little tidbits I've picked up after listening in on the office coffee clutches.

"You sure about that? Since you've been working on one and only one project for days on end and haven't come to a satisfactory conclusion?"

Ugh, where does he get off? The gloves are off now. To hell with him, and to hell with Ryland for guilting me into playing nice for his sake! I like him, I really do, and I enjoy working with him, but I won't let this asshat talk to me like I'm some idiot off the street who doesn't deserve respect, just because he's rich and thinks he's a big deal. "I have an idea. Why don't you try to fix this yourself, since you're such a know-it-all?"

"Sam!" Ryland barks. "That's enough."

"No, no, I want to hear what Mr. Cage has to say," I reply, never looking away from Lincoln's eyes. They're not bad eyes. Deep, dark, stormy, mysterious; the sort of eyes I would enjoy staring into if they weren't in his face. But they are, which means they suck.

His full and in any other circumstances, totally kissable mouth curves up in a sneer. "You don't bark after you buy a dog. I hire people like you to do that sort of thing for me, so I'm freed up to focus on big-picture issues, which you would understand if you were in my position."

And damn my mouth for speaking faster than my brain can think, because what comes out of my mouth next is beneath me, "Big-picture issues like the fact that your daughter is asleep in the next room? What a wonderful, professional atmosphere you've cultivated here."

The silence in the room is ominous.

Even Ryland can't back me up this time. I wish I could go back in time and not have said those words, because it was unfair of me to throw that in his face. I don't know anything about his personal life. I only know what Ryland told me on our way past the conference room...that his six-year-old daughter showed up out of nowhere earlier in the day.

It could be a trick of the light, but Lincoln's face seems to change color. It's goes to roughly the same shade as an eggplant and his eyes burn like two coals. "Congratulations," he says coldly. "You just crossed the line, Ms. Harper. And you're roughly five seconds away from getting fired."

"All right, all right, let's all be calm here," Ryland implores, stepping between us.

"Nobody talks about my kid that way, especially when they have no clue what the hell they're talking about," he snarls, glaring over Ryland's shoulder at me.

I'm almost tempted to apologize. Almost. But there's something about this man. I know I did wrong, but I cannot bring myself to apologize.

"Understood," Ryland replies, shooting me a warning look over his shoulder. "She should know better than to say things like that."

But I can't stop myself. "What about what he was saying?" I ask.

"Like what? Like how you should get your act together and make the drone work without bursting into flames?" Lincoln taunts.

RIVER LAURENT

"Get my act together?" I can feel my blood start to boil. "Perhaps if it had been designed better, this wouldn't be a problem."

"There is nothing wrong with the design," Ryland says to the two of us. "We just have to figure out how to solve the problem. There's always a way to solve a problem, but we can't waste time with stupid, petty fighting. Remember, we're all on the same team."

Boy, he's just the king of the pep talks. And I thought I was the only person whose butt got smoke blown up it. As it turns out, he's been practicing on Lincoln for all these years. No wonder he's so good at it. "If I'm going to solve this problem, I need uninterrupted work time," I interject in an attempt to break the tension. "I need a little faith, a little more time, and a little leeway."

"You've been given plenty of time," Lincoln reminds me.

"Thanks. I completely forgot."

Ryland scowls at me, but I don't back down. "There are other things I can do. I know I'm real close and I'm not one to give up. Ever."

Lincoln's lips purse as he considers this. "You have that going for you, at least."

"That's only for starters," I murmur.

"Yes, well, I'll believe that when I see it. For now, I only have your word and this guy's assurance that hiring you wasn't the biggest mistake of his and my life."

Something tells me he's made much bigger mistakes—such as his marriage—but even I am not stupid enough to pursue that topic. "That's just fine by me. You'll see for yourself once I've solved the problem that the other departments have gotten me into."

Muscles jump in his jaw as my dig hits home. He turns to Ryland. "You'd better leave. Now."

"Yeah. I was thinking the same thing," Ryland says, as he grabs my arm, leading me out of the office and down the hall.

I'm so relieved at having an excuse to leave Lincoln's presence without being the first person to back down from our fight that it doesn't even occur to me to ask my manager to get his hands off me.

He doesn't let go until we're inside the elevator with the doors closed tight behind us. He sighs heavily, seeming to deflate before my very eyes. "What do you think you're trying to do? Do you think you can mouth off like that and still have a job when all is said and done?"

"It seems like I do still have a job," I point out with a shaky laugh.

He's not impressed, judging from the way he scowls. "Barely. Thanks to me. Once again."

I bite my lip. "I'm grateful, Ryland. Really, I am. I never normally behave like that. I don't know why, but he annoys me so much."

"I warned you," he mutters, rubbing the bridge of his nose with his thumb and forefinger. "I warned you, I did everything but beg you to avoid running your mouth in there. And that crack about Maddie! Oh, my God, I couldn't believe it."

"I shouldn't have said it," I admit, blushing. "It was low."

"Lower than low," he agrees.

"I can't stand him. I know he's your friend and you mean a lot to each other, but I really can't stand him."

"And that means absolutely nothing. Christ, how old are you, anyway?"

"Old enough to know what you're saying," I mumble. I take a deep breath and have a reality check. "It doesn't matter if I like my boss. He's still my boss, and I ought to respect him."

"Right and right," he replies, nodding his head almost comically.

"I just don't like getting pushed too hard," I admit. "And he pushed me. Maybe because it's already so hard as a woman—"

"Don't give me that sexual inequality, mansplaining, mumbo jumbo right now."

"Hold up. Mansplaining mumbo jumbo?" I ask, hands on my hips.

"You know what I mean," he groans as we step off the elevator. "I mean that it's no excuse for your behavior. And I'm not always going to be around to save your job for you. I shouldn't have to babysit you."

"All I'm trying to say is I've had to fight hard for respect in my profession."

"And you get it. From me. And you will from him too, but you'll have to earn it. I know you can save the day. Don't screw it all up by saying things you can't take back. Okay?"

I nod, resigned and exhausted. Maybe it's time to call it a day. I can worry about Lincoln Cage in the morning. And every day thereafter until I fix this issue.

Lucky, lucky me.

SAMANTHA

"You've been working too hard, dear. It's a good thing for you to take the evening off and visit with family." I don't think Sophia has strung that many words together in my presence in all the years she's been married to my father. Wife Number Four is by far my least favorite, and that's saying something.

"I'm just glad to have the opportunity," I reply with a smile so tight, I'm surprised my teeth don't crack. It's absolutely ridiculous, the whole charade we go through every month. My monthly visit to my father's house for dinner. A dinner which, if history serves, I won't be able to digest without the help of antacids. Who could enjoy a meal eaten in a mausoleum, because that's exactly how it feels to sit here with these people at their ridiculous, sixteen-seat dinner table which only holds four of us.

My father looks distracted, as always. We haven't even made eye contact since I arrived. He'd have to look up from his phone in order for that to happen. Back in the day, it used to be the newspaper which ate up his attention. Now I can see his face, but it doesn't improve anything. Now, I just get to watch him actively avoid looking at me.

Sophia has spent the entire meal picking at her food, shuffling it around on her plate. I don't think I've ever seen her eat a proper meal, or even a proper course unless it involves a thin soup or dry salad. No wonder she always looks and sounds irritable, even when she's trying to be polite.

Veronica, on the other hand, never bothers trying for politeness. My beloved stepsister. The lazy brat. She swings her wavy hair extensions over one shoulder, running the tip of her tongue over her glossy lips before asking, "Don't you get paid at this job of yours? The one you were so thrilled about the last time you were here?"

"Aw, Ronnie, it's so nice of you to remember our last dinner together."

Her cheeks flame red. She hates that nickname. "Just because you like to be called Sam doesn't mean we all enjoy being mistaken for men."

"Oh, sweetie. Nobody could ever mistake you for a man," her mother interjects.

Right. Not with the ridiculous implants she got a few months ago. Does she really think nobody noticed her going from a flat chest to a C-cup? It wasn't even a subtle difference. But then, she's never been one for subtlety. She applies her makeup with a putty knife, for God's sake.

"Anyway, as I was saying," she continues, nostrils flaring. "I wondered if you got paid any decent money, since you still haven't bought any decent clothes."

"Some of us pay our own rent and bills," I remind her,

keeping my voice as sweet as I can. "We can't all live with our parents."

"Maybe if you were good enough to run Daddy's company, you'd have a half-decent wardrobe."

That's it. I've been trying. I really have. All these years of her digs, her insinuations, her reminders that I don't have a boyfriend or a husband. I've managed to avoid unleashing on her all this time, but I'm still smarting from my encounter with Lincoln and my inability to find a solution to the drone problem. "He's not your daddy, for one thing," I remind her coldly.

"But he is, dear," Sophia insists, her eyes sparkling as she rides to her daughter's rescue. As always. She smooths both hands over her perfectly coiffed, bleached hair while explaining, "I've encouraged her to refer to him as her father, after all."

"She's nearly my age. Don't you think it's a little late for her second childhood?" I ask, the meal long forgotten. Not like I was missing much, anyway. At least we had a decent cook while I was living in this monstrosity of a house with its eight-thousand square feet and indoor grotto and a million features that are completely unnecessary for a home only three people live in. It's like a wax museum, complete with Sophia, the Waxwork.

"Now, now, girls." Sophia chuckles ditzily, glancing at my father who hasn't looked up from his phone screen. "Let's not fight and ruin the evening. We see each other so rarely."

And this is why. I can barely care at this point. It's all a farce, a pitiful attempt at making us look like a family. We're not. I've never felt like part of them and never will. We're just different types of people. Sometimes, I wish they would leave me alone and allow me to live the rest of my life in peace. I wouldn't mind never having to lay eyes on this ugly, ornate wallpaper again. I'd never have to touch my lips to the heavy, crystal wine goblets or get a headache from my stepmother's cloyingly sweet perfume ever again. It would be glorious.

But it's impossible, because I can't imagine not having any family at all. Even a bad, distant, disappointed father is better than none at all.

"Don't worry, Mommy," Veronica croons, flashing her mother a fake smile. "Nothing she has to say upsets me. I'd be a nasty old maid, too, if I were her."

I have to let go of my goblet before it makes contact with the side of her head. "Is that silicone in your chest, or did all the air from your head move downward?"

Her gasp would put even the hammiest actress to shame. "How dare you?" she demands, jumping up from the table and spilling red wine all over the pristine linen.

It soaks in, reminding me of blood. I'm not usually so morbid, but I watched a movie last night where a man was killed on a snow-covered ground. "Do you really think anybody would think those things are real?" I ask curiously, gesturing to her chest.

"You bitch!" Instead of flinging her water in my face, which I was almost sure she would, she storms out of the dining room with Sophia at her heels. I can hear their shoes click-clacking across the tile floors, reminding me of horse hooves. Veronica's demands that I leave immediately floating over it all.

I sigh, resting against the high-backed chair. It's just me and Dad now, and it might as well be me alone. He's oblivious. I wonder if he heard anything that just took place.

As it turns out, he did. "I hope you're proud of yourself, young lady." He sounds so bored, I'm surprised he doesn't yawn outright.

"I don't know. I thought the comment about Veronica's implants was pretty good."

My dad has no sense of humor. He looks at me for the first time and frowns. "Be that as it may, you have no right to speak to your stepsister that way. You know how it upsets Sophia."

"We wouldn't want that, would we?" *What about me?* I want to ask with all my heart, want to let the question pour out of me along with all the pain of his absence from my life. Why don't I matter? Why haven't I ever mattered? It doesn't even make a difference that I studied what I did and made a career where I have in the hopes of earning his respect?

He folds his hands on the table, looking me square in the eye. When he does, I almost wish he'd go back to his emails or whatever it is he's been engrossed in. "Veronica does make a good point," he claims, looking me up and down. "If your boss over at Guardian Technologies thought you were worthwhile, he'd pay you enough to allow you to dress your-self up a little."

As always, I feel myself shrinking into my own skin. Wishing I could hide from his critical stare. Those icy eyes, so light, they're nearly clear. They see right into my soul, touching my insecurities one-by-one until I'm raw and directionless while wondering again, why I even care what he thinks. He certainly doesn't give a shit about my thoughts.

"I'm a Senior Engineer," I remind him with all the dignity I can muster.

"A title, and a title only," he dismisses, shaking his head. "Samantha, it's best you drop the pretense now, rather than allowing it to drag out until you're too old for any man to want you."

"I don't care if no man—"

"Every woman with sense cares about that," he cuts me off irritably. "You're still an attractive girl. Stop wasting your time. It isn't as if someone with your limited abilities would ever come up with some groundbreaking development."

"How would you even know the first thing about my abilities?" I whisper, disappointment threatening to choke me. And how is it that he manages to remind me so much of Lincoln Cage? Didn't he also doubt my abilities?

"You are my daughter, my flesh and blood, so of course, I love you, but that doesn't blind me to the reality of this business. I know what I am talking about. You don't have what it takes to survive in the difficult business environment you have chosen."

"How can you be so cruel?"

"Perhaps because I have little respect for people who insist on wedging themselves in places where they are unwanted. We both know you've been determined to take over my company since you were a teenager, regardless of whether or not you were ever considered for the position. Which you weren't," he adds, as though he needs to. "I never had any intention of naming you as my successor, but you insisted on being undignified and struggling to curry favor. It's all very unseemly."

"Unseemly?" I gasp. Tears burn behind my eyes, but stay unshed as I stand with all the dignity I can muster. Holding my head high, I look down on him. This man is my father, but I do not know him and he does not know me. Any love he might have felt for me dissolved when his marriage to my mother did. If they'd stayed together, I might have, but as it was I never had a chance.

He has never loved me.

He forced her to give him custody to punish her. I don't blame her for running away, clear to the other side of the planet. I would've done the same thing in her place.

"Well, Father. You are wrong. I *never*, not one instant, wanted to take over your company, I just want *your* company. I wanted you to love me." My voice breaks and I know, I cannot stay another moment here. "Don't worry I won't sully your perfect domesticity with my unseemliness. I'm leaving, and I won't be back for another dinner, or anything else."

"Yeah, like the times you threatened to run away when you were four, six, nine, and fifteen. You'll come crawling back. You always do," he scoffs, reaching for his knife and fork.

I watch him cut a piece of steak, completely unconcerned. "No. Not this time I won't," I swear.

He lifts his glass of red wine as if in a toast and that mocking gesture is too much.

I turn on my heel and run out of his mansion. I manage to hold back my tears until I've slid behind the wheel of my car.

I know the way down the wide, graveled driveway well enough to navigate it with wet, blurry eyes. I don't stop until I'm off the property, pulling over on the shoulder of the road and putting the car in park before folding my arms over the wheel and crying my heart out.

How could anybody be so cruel? How can a man look at his daughter, his actual flesh and blood, and talk to her the way he talks to me? Is it the blow to his pride when I demanded to live on my own, without his help? I would rather die than let him control a single aspect of my life. He wasn't nice to me even when I lived under his roof. Every wife he brought home to compete with me and make me feel small. In the end, I couldn't stand it anymore.

"Damn him to hell. I'll never go back there again," I sob to the otherwise empty car.

At least, I won't have to pretend to be nice to my step-relatives again. The thought isn't a bad one really, and it's almost enough to soothe me into pulling myself together enough to drive home.

Then, at the last minute, I steer the car in the direction of the office. "We'll see just how impossible it is for me to come up with a breakthrough," I mutter with renewed determination.

LINCOLN

"**D**addy?"

I look up from the piles of papers on the desk at my daughter, cozy in the nest she's built herself in the corner of my office. The kid is self-reliant, I'll give her that. She keeps herself busy, knows how to pass the time without being a drain on my limited mental bandwidth.

"Mm hmm?"

"Do you work late like this all the time?" She stifles a yawn.

I didn't realize it was even as late as it is. A glance at the clock tells me it's nearly ten-thirty. "I'm sorry, kiddo. No, I don't do this all the time." Lies and more lies. "It's a really busy time right now, like we talked about when you first came to live with me."

She nods solemnly, curls bouncing. "Yeah. You have to show your prototop."

It's an effort to keep a straight face. "Close enough. Prototype."

"Right." She looks down, mouthing the word as though to commit it to memory for the next time she wants to use it.

Those little quirks in her personality are what endear her to me the most. I love her simply for the fact that she's alive, of course, but there's more to it. As much of a pain in the ass as it's been to work things out up to this point, Regina did me an incalculably massive favor. I'd already missed too much of my daughter's life.

I push back from the desk, stretching my arms over my head. I recognize my workaholic tendencies. To this point, I've had the luxury of devoting my entire life to building the business. After losing custody of her it was a wonderful outlet for me to pour everything I had into the business, instead of sinking into a profound depression.

I haven't really had the time to sit down and think of what life would look like with Maddie in the picture. Obviously, I can't raise her in this office. It's all right for a few days, maybe a week—and even then, it's not very all right. It's just an emergency measure. She'll need stability, structure, the right to a normal childhood. The only blessing in Regina's timing is that she waited until summer to do this. If I had to negotiate a new school, books and supplies, homework and projects from the first day, I would've lost my mind.

There is a ringing tone sounding from the princess tent.

Maddie's eyes grow round as she grabs her pink phone. "Oh, oh, it's Mommy," she announces and scrambles back deep into the tent. "Hello, Mommy," she greets.

"Hello darling," Regina says cheerfully. "What's the time there now?"

"Uh… it's nearly bedtime."

"Right. Are you having a good time with your father?"

"Yes."

"Really?" Regina sounds surprised.

"Yes," Maddie says again.

"You mean your father is spending time with you?"

"Daddy is with me all the time."

"Really? Don't you have a nanny?"

"No."

"I see. Why it is so dark there?"

"I'm in my tent."

"Are you in your bedroom?"

I close my eyes. Fuck, here comes trouble.

"Um…Yes, yes, I am," Maddie lies.

I open my eyes in shock.

"Are you having a good time Mommy?"

Her mother starts to regale her with a story of what she is getting up to. Apparently, they are in France and just finished watching a polo match. She starts telling her how she met Prince Harry and I tune out and think of my daughter. No matter what, tomorrow, we have to get the paints for her room, because next week I am going to start looking for a nanny for her. Tonight is the last night she is spending on the floor of my office.

"Good night, Mommy."

"Good night, darling. I'll call you again in a few days."

I stand up and walk over to the tent entrance.

Maddie pops her head out of the entrance again.

"Maddie, why did you lie to your mother about being in your own room?"

She shrugs and looks down.

"You don't have to lie, you know. You can tell the truth."

"But Daddy you don't understand. Mommy will be mad with you if I tell her."

"So let her be. I'll deal with her. I don't want you telling lies to protect me, okay?"

She frowns.

"Did you hear what I said, Maddie?"

She looks at me anxiously. "Daddy, what if Mommy becomes so mad with you she takes me back to live with her and Juan?"

The world is such a different place for a child. It becomes a helpless pawn too easily. I smile softly at her. "Remember when the Judge decided that you were too young to live with me?"

She nods.

"Well, the Judge decided you are old enough to live with me now and he signed a paper that says so. I have it in my desk if you want to see it. And that means nobody can take you away from me now. Not even Mommy. Unless you want to go back to her."

"I love Mommy, but I think I'll stay with you, Daddy."

"Good. Now, can we agree that you won't tell lies again, for no good reason?"

"It was a good reason," she insists.

"Maddie," I say warningly.

"All right," she agrees with a sigh. Sometimes, she seems wise beyond her years, but hand shy, like a beaten dog.

I firmly doubt Regina would've ever laid a hand on her, but there are ways to hurt a kid without hitting them. Like ignoring them or treating them like a nuisance. My blood boils at the idea. "So anyway, we are going to paint your room this weekend," I say.

She brightens instantly, her eyes shining. "We are?"

"Yes, I'll get Erica to buy all the paints tomorrow. You can choose the colors you want and we'll have a go at doing up your room on Saturday, okay?"

She nods happily.

I stroke her head. God, I love this kid.

"Do you do a lot of fun things, Daddy?" she asks, resting her chin in her palm, and looking up at me with those heart-melting eyes.

"What's your idea of fun things?"

"I like eating Nutella."

I laugh. "Yeah?"

"Yeah. I wish I could eat it for breakfast, lunch and dinner. I dream of eating Nutella."

Now, I'm really laughing. "You dream of eating Nutella?"

"Mmmm."

"Okay, I'll make sure we have some Nutella back in the apartment. Now what else do you like to do?"

"Oh, I don't know." She shrugs and looks at her bare toes.

I can remember the first time I saw her. It was her toes that completely stunned me. They were like a row of corn kernels. So neat, so tiny, so unimaginably perfect. "Maddie?" I prompt.

She looks up. "Yeah?"

"I asked you a question. What fun things do you like to do?"

She sucks her bottom lip into her mouth. I can see her thinking. As if I had asked her a trick question.

"I wanna know. Really," I say softly.

"I like…museums," she ventures, nearly whispering.

I grin. "You do? Me, too."

A spark of light flickers in her eyes. "Really?"

"Sure, I do. Do you like art? History? Science? I like science, myself."

"Yeah, me too! But Mommy doesn't like them. She says only boys like those kinds of boring things." She sits up a little straighter against the pillow wedged between her back and the wall. "But I like history stuff too. Like the dinosaurs. I went to a dinosaur exhibit with my class last year and it was sooooooo awesome."

"We'll have to find more things like that to go to," I offer. "And amusement parks, if you like them. Do you?"

"Yeah!" Though her illness hasn't completely passed, she looks more alive and energetic than I've seen her thus far. It takes so little to make a kid happy.

"I have an idea," I venture, folding my hands on the desk and looking at her very seriously. "Make a list of all the fun things you like to do, or things you want to do, but have never had the chance yet. And we'll start checking things off together. Deal?"

"Deal!" She immediately closes out the app she's been playing with and opens a text document.

Watching her enthusiasm makes me smile. Kids these days. More confident with technology than most adults.

Now that she's occupied, I use the opportunity to get back to work. I'm not crazy about the presentation that's been put together for the demo, and it's killing me to keep from micromanaging the team in charge of organizing things, but I have enough on my plate at the moment. I need to trust my employees. At least, that's what Ryland keeps telling me.

My employees. That thought leads me down a path I've traveled many times in the last two days, to that meeting with Sam. It's rare for me to wish I could go back and do something over, but that night is one of those instances. Everything went wrong, beginning to end.

I hate it when I lose control in tense situations, but I did. I'm supposed to be the guy who keeps his cool. I need to be.

People rely on me for employment. It's my job to keep it together when the rest of the world is falling apart.

So, the fact that some kid fresh out of college, some brash thing who's still just trying out her sexuality, got under my skin to the point where I exploded and blurted out those sharp, harsh comments is unsettling. Even embarrassing.

Brash thing or not, she managed to drop a truth in my lap that's even more unsettling—the fact that I might be perceived as a leader who sits in his office, waiting for answers, expecting others to fix problems while I tell them to hurry up, do it better, etcetera. Her dig that I should fix the bug in the drone myself if I knew so much, sticks in my craw like I cannot describe.

Even now, her attitude and her accusation stings just as freshly as it did when she first hurled it at me. That's saying something, since it stung my ego in a pretty big way at the time.

A soft snore catches my attention, pushing thoughts of Sam from my mind. Maddie fell asleep while making up her list, the pillow under her head on the floor. I hope she's dreaming of all the wonderful things we'll do together. My brow furrows when I take in the full sight, however—my little girl, asleep on the office floor with a pile of blankets arranged beneath her.

I sigh.

This is the way things have to be for just a little while. I'll do better for her when the pressure's off. It just happens to be especially heavy at the moment. I wish Sam would hurry the hell up with the bug fix, since that's one of the two over-riding issues taking up the most room in my mind right now.

The other is the Weismann thievery and the leak in my organization. I need a break more than ever.

Maybe it's time for me to put my money where my mouth is. I can't do anything about the leak just yet, but I can try to fix the overheating problem. What will Sam think when she comes into the lab tomorrow and finds that I've been messing around in her work? I'd hate it, but...

What the hell do I care?

Before I know it, I'm lifting Maddie and her bedding as gently as possible and carrying everything down the hall, into the elevator and down to the lab. I'll show her that I can be a team player. I'm no dictator, expecting my minions to do my bidding without complaint or even assistance from their leader. I'm not above rolling up my sleeves and going into the trenches.

Evidently, I'm not alone in this.

The first thing I hear while unlocking and opening the door is a gasp.

LINCOLN

"I didn't expect anybody to be here," I whisper, looking down at Maddie before meeting Sam's gaze.

She's flustered, one hand clasped over her chest. "Sorry. I didn't expect to see anyone, either."

"Especially not me, huh?"

Her cheeks burn with a deep pink, and she ducks her head to tuck long strands of blonde hair behind both ears.

The clock on the wall tells me it's now past midnight, but she's here. I can't help the swell of grudging admiration which comes up when I consider her dedication. She wasn't just shooting her mouth off when she claimed to be working hard on this issue. Once again, I feel like I was more than a bit unfair to her. She's doing her best with a problem that got dropped in her lap, unceremoniously too.

She smiles when she catches sight of Maddie and her eyes soften somewhat. "Beautiful," she whispers.

"Thank you." I look around, now doubtful. "I had hoped to

make a little bed up for her down here so she can sleep, but—"

Sam gets up, waving her hands. "I'll help you out. Here. Give me those."

I loosen my grip a bit, enough for her to work the blankets out from between my arms and Maddie's body, and she shakes them out before arranging them in a far corner of the lab, behind filing cabinets and tucked away from the rest of the workspace. I crouch beside her, placing my daughter on the makeshift bed while Sam turns out the nearby lights to give her a bit more darkness.

"Thanks," I whisper as I stand. I look down at my daughter once more. She is fast asleep. At least, her presence will keep the two of us from killing each other. I hope. I turn away to get down to business.

"What are you still doing here with her?" she whispers once we're out of earshot.

Just like that, her way with words brings my blood to a simmer. "What exactly do you think I should do? Leave her at home by herself? Or maybe I should let her sleep in the car, out in the garage. I'll crack the windows in case it gets too hot in there."

She flushes a deep red, but holds my gaze with a defiant lift of her chin. "I didn't mean to insinuate any wrongdoing. I was only asking. It's so late."

"No kidding. I thought it was midday."

Her eyes flash with temper. "Wow. The later the night gets, the worse your temper is."

"I could say the same for you." Then, I look down at the work she's been doing and instantly regret my lapse into bitterness. Once again, my mouth has run away from me before I had the chance to think twice. The girl is here well after everyone has gone home for the night, but all I can do is take her semi-innocent questions and turn them into something negative.

"I'm happy to go home, if that's what you want," she says in a fierce whisper, though I get the impression from the way she's planted her feet that she has no intention of going anywhere.

I jerk my chin in the direction of her work. "What's happening here?"

"The usual thrills and chills," she replies. "I had an idea tonight while I was on my way from dinner and wanted to try it out."

"Dinner?" Does she have a boyfriend? She's dressed pretty nicely, I now notice. A slim-fitting skirt, a silk blouse which simultaneously covers up and promises so much from her full, firm breasts. Patent leather heels make her legs look longer. I don't want to come across as a perv, but I have to keep from licking my lips at the sight of them. She's too damn tempting. Every inch of her smooth skin calls to me. I frown. It's not right, thinking about her this way. Maybe it's because she gets my blood up and then my mind goes in directions it shouldn't.

My attention snaps back to her face, and I'm glad she's focused on the components spread over the table rather than on the assessment, I just performed on her body. She has me all mixed up. An uncomfortable feeling.

65

"Yes," she murmurs, shaking her head, still focused on the components she's piecing together. "Dinner with the family. A monthly torture ritual."

I snort softly, and out of more than a little relief. It's none of my business whether this girl has a boyfriend or not and I know it, but I still prefer the thought of a tense family meal to a romantic night out. I don't know why. "Family's rarely ever easy," I commiserate.

"Mine more than most," she says.

I catch the real sadness behind the glib comment. I stare at her intrigued.

"What about you?" she asks quickly.

"What about me?"

"Tense dinners? Or do you have that perfect family where everybody gets together and lobs jokes across the table before drinking cocoa by the fire?"

Her image makes me wince, since it's so close to the way things used to be. "Not so much anymore," I murmur, remembering Mom's dinners and the holidays we spent together. Even though it was just the three of us, the house couldn't have been fuller with love if we'd tried. It's enough to bring a lump to my throat.

"I'm sorry," she sighs. "That was insensitive."

I glance across to find her stricken expression. "It's all right. Really. And no dinners, tense or otherwise here."

"Well. You aren't missing much," she murmurs with a wry smile. "Honestly, after what I went through, I had to come here to work out some of my frustration."

"Most people would go to a gym to work their frustration out," I say, watching her long, slim and sure fingers work. She's intimately aware of the hardware she is handling, operating without hesitation. As if the bits and pieces are extensions of her. There's something seductive about watching a person so completely in-tune with what they're doing—especially when it's something I designed. I know instinctively that she'd slap my hand away if I dared encroach on what she sees as her territory."

"Working out is okay, especially if I'm punching something," she admits. "But I find this even more stimulating. Exhilarating too, when I manage to work out the solution to a problem."

"I've been there."

She lifts her head and looks at me. "Oh, yeah?"

"Sure. You focus all attention on making something work. You put your heart and soul into it, trying everything you can think of. Calling on all your skill. And when it works and you were right?" I smile. "It's an unbelievable high. You feel ten feet tall."

She smiles back. Her whole face transforming. "I can't think of anything better," she says softly.

God, she's beautiful. "I can think of one or two things," I mutter under my breath, but obviously audible if the way color floods her cheeks is any indication. I have to stop this, and now. All I need is for her to call me up on charges of sexual harassment and I'm in hot water. The last thing I need with my daughter in my charge. "What did you tweak?" I ask, desperate to get off the subject of sex or innuendo.

She snaps the last piece into place. Before me on the table, is a fully-assembled drone. "I added a thin insulation blanket around the battery casing and an extra layer of heat paste behind the motherboard," she explains. "It might keep the heat from frying anything out."

My mind drops into design mood. "You think that'll do it, huh?"

"It can't hurt, can it? Nothing I've done so far has made much of a difference. Good luck, Barry," she says.

"You called the drone, Barry?"

She avoids my eyes as she hits the timer. "It's just for ease of reference."

I try not smile. We sit in silence for six-and-a-half minutes as the drone makes its circular flight over our heads. Both of us hoping against hope that something will change and the drone will stay in flight. When it keeps running, we look at each other with wide, hopeful eyes. This could be it. This could be the breakthrough.

It isn't.

Once we reach the seventh minute mark, the sickeningly familiar sequence of events begins, with the temperature readout spiking. The engine sputters out and I land the drone before it can crash.

"Damn!" Her head sinks into her arms, crossed on the table.

"I'm sorry." And I am, and for more than just me or the company. Her passion is evident, as is her dedication. The girl drove in after dinner, when she could've gone home like a normal person and living a normal life, but she came here, instead. And she's devastated by her lack of progress.

"You're sorry?" she asks, dismayed. "This is your baby, and I'm still screwing it up."

"This isn't my baby," I point out, then jerk a thumb in the direction of my sleeping daughter. "That is. This is just work."

She raises an eyebrow, smirking ever so slightly. "Why don't I believe that?"

"What do you mean?"

"If you weren't as crazy devoted to this as I am, you wouldn't still be here. You're just as invested in that baby," she jerks her thumb in the direction the drone. "As any of us in development."

"Of course. But even so, I know you're working hard and I know you're frustrated. I'm just glad you haven't given up yet. I'm not sure where we would be if you did."

"I can tell you where we'd be." She chuckles mirthlessly. "We'd be in the same spot we were in when this was dumped in my lap, because I haven't gotten anywhere."

"That's not true," I point out, indicating her notes. "We know what doesn't work. All we have to do is find what does. You've made tremendous progress."

She eyes me suspiciously, like an animal unsure whether it should trust the man with the gun who says he's not a hunter.

I make an effort to keep my expression neutral in order to convince her I mean what I say.

"Thanks," she finally murmurs, tucking her hair back.

It must be a nervous gesture when she is unsure what to do with those crafty hands of hers. I can't help but wonder what else they're capable of…"Wait a second. What about the fan casing?"

"What about it?" she asks, watching as I turn the drone upside down.

I point to the semi-circular cutouts in the drone's exterior, which allow hot air to flow from inside the body the way a computer's fan does. "What if these were wider and that piece there was moved here? Not by much, but enough to draw out more heat at a time? That might make a big enough difference."

She purses her generous mouth, eyes narrowing, as she processes the idea in her mind. "That could help. We've already improved flight time. If we keep going in this direction, it could be enough."

I immediately begin to disassemble the drone, leaving replacing the circuitry to her while I use an awl to widen the openings. There's something nice about working alongside someone for once. A camaraderie I've missed out on for a long time. I find myself smiling, even as the night rolls on and sleep becomes a distant concept. I'll be a mess come morning, but it'll be worth it if we can score a win.

"All right. I think this will do it. Any larger, and the integrity of the case will be lost." I hand the last piece over.

Sam works it into place, completing the drone once again. She grins at me. A real smile.

I'm almost transfixed by it.

"Okay. Here goes nothing." She starts the drone and keeps it hovering just inches from the table surface.

We both study the readouts from the internal systems as the minutes pass—minutes which seem to stretch out into eternity. So much hangs in the balance I don't even want to think about it.

"It's already better at three minutes than it's ever been," she whispers, a thread of excitement evident as she jabs a finger at the screen. "See?"

"I see," I whisper, willing myself not to allow excitement to enter into this. I can't get ahead of myself. I can't allow that. Even so, I can't help but feel hopeful when four, then five, then six minutes pass with little change in the temperature of the processor.

"Oh, my God," she breathes, chewing her thumbnail, barely blinking as she continues to monitor the numbers.

I don't say anything, just stare at the monitor. The temperature holds steady.

"Seven minutes. I think we've done it. I really do. This is it! I know it."

"Let's wait and see," I caution, though I feel anything but cautious myself. Seven minutes. Eight. Nine. By the time we hit ten and the temperature still hangs well within the acceptable range, my heart is nearly pounding out of my chest.

"We did it," she cries, clasping her hands together and jumping up and down like a child.

"I think you're right," I'm finally ready to admit. I turn my eyes to her with a big grin on my face. "Fucking hell, Sam. I think you're right, I think we did it."

She flaps her hands in front of her face like she's trying to hold back her emotion, and I see now just how much this has meant to her. She's spent so many hours devoting all of her skill and intelligence to this single project, and to see it come to fruition is too much for her to handle. I've been there. I'm there right now, myself.

I do the only thing that feels good and right, and that's pulling her to me for a tight hug. She throws her arms around my neck, trembling with delirious relief and probably more than a little exhaustion, seeing as how it's now after three in the morning and we're both half-dead—but elated. Elated in the way people are who haven't worked together on something for a long, long time and have finally achieved success will never understand. The taste of victory is like heady wine. So potent it wipes out everything but that moment. Nothing else exists. Just that moment in time.

It gets the better of me.

Or maybe I can blame the way her neck moves and the intoxicating smell of her perfume floods my nostrils, seducing me, making me press my lips against her warm, inviting mouth at this late hour. And she can blame the way she kisses me back—hard, desperately hard, breathless and crushing her lips to mine—on her … elation.

SAMANTHA

Wait. What are we doing?

I jerk my head back. "But I don't even like you," I gasp.

"No, I don't like you much either, but what the hell," he mutters, and his mouth crashes down on mine again.

Yup, I don't like him, but I sure do like the way his lips move over mine, the way he holds me tight enough to take my breath away. His arms are as strong as they look and firm with bulging muscle. The sort of arms I could lose myself in and never come up for air and be perfectly fine with it because oh, my God, he's the best kisser I've ever known.

My toes curl and my arms break out in goosebumps as the sensations from his probing, demanding tongue race through my body, leaving me trembling—eager for more.

But this is wrong. It's so wrong.

He's my boss, for Christ's sake. I shouldn't even be thinking about this, much less doing it. But here we are, and I want this. I want it so much. I can't think about it, or else the magic will dissolve.

Anyway, it feels right, my body pressed against his, my hands running up and down his arms, shoulders and back. God, he's perfect, the most perfect body I've ever touched. I can't get enough of him. He pushes me against the wall and I have no choice, but to succumb. Not that I want to do anything else.

I pull my mouth from his for a split second, though, remembering the little one. She's hidden from view, only the edges of her blankets visible from behind the file cabinets. Even so, when I cut my eyes in that direction, he nods.

"Shh..." Then his mouth is plundering mine again, and the kiss is deeper, more passionate this time. Actually, all-consuming. I feel myself melting, turning to nothing but a puddle of sheer ecstatic pleasure as he kisses away every last inhibition I harbor.

We sink to the floor, wrapped up in each other. He stretches his tall frame out over mine while one hand slides up my leg from ankle to thigh. Only the knowledge of the sleeping child on the other side of the lab keeps me from crying out my pleasure. From begging him for more. His fingers dance at the hem of my panties, teasing both of us, while his mouth kisses a trail from my lips to my chin, down my throat, to the bit of skin revealed above the buttons of my blouse. I work at them with trembling fingers, ready to burst with need.

He chuckles against my skin, sending pleasurable little vibrations through me as he moves lower and lower with each new open button. He works my shirt out of my skirt, opening it fully, one of his hands cupping my breast through my bra and squeezing gently, his tongue sliding beneath the lace. I hold his head close, my fingers tangling in his hair, arching my back in an attempt to give myself to him, to present myself for him to feast on. He rolls his hips in response, driving his bulge against my thigh, and we both groan softly.

"Fuck," he curses under his breath. "I don't have any condoms."

I sit up halfway, shedding the blouse and unhooking my bra. "I do." I reach up to the tabletop and pull my purse down. I extract a flat packet out and tear the silver wrapper away.

He's on me in an instant, sucking at my nipples until the ache between my legs is almost painful. He works my skirt up to my hips and slides my panties off, tossing them aside and spreading my thighs wide to reveal my wet, tender slit.

The growl, low and deep in his throat, precedes the dipping of his fingers into my folds.

I grip his shoulders tight, wishing I could scream as my hips buck against his hand. He works my clit, breathing hard against my neck, both of us struggling to give into our passion while staying as quiet as possible.

If anything, that only makes this even more forbidden. And hotter, so much hotter.

It's inappropriate. Actually, it's not inappropriate—it's wrong for me to have sex with the boss! It's against *every* rule. Everything about this is just downright wrong. The way he strokes my clit, the way his fingers slide inside me. The way my muscles clench around the thick digits. The way he pumps them in and out until I'm unable to stop myself as my mouth opens in a cry of pleasure. His hand clamps down over my mouth, and my eyes go wide with surprise, but I don't pull away. In fact, I jerk my hips toward him, thrusting right back. Until I dissolve in a frenzy of furious spasms, biting on the side of his fist to quiet my scream of ecstasy.

I'm still panting when I hear his zipper. He sheaths himself and I feel the heavy weight of his erect dick against my thigh. I glance down. My eyes open with surprise and lustful hunger as I note the length and girth. I want to draw him into me, hold him fast, take every last bit of pleasure I can.

He spreads my legs wider. Grabbing one of my tits, he takes it into his mouth. He bites down on it as he thrusts the massive head of his cock into me. "You're so hot and wet," he grunts, as my nipple pops out of his mouth.

I close my eyes and bite my lip as I adjust to his size.

"And so fucking tight," he hisses between clenched teeth.

My pussy clenches. He withdraws only to drive forward again. And again. He takes my other nipple and bites down hard. I open my mouth and his hand clamps down just as he rams into me. It's a rough fuck. His cock enormous and angry inside me, his eyes watching my pussy, open wide for him to use; and his hands…they roam where they please.

With a dark glint in his eyes, he possess me, claims me, and brands me.

I pull him down until he's on his forearms. Opening his shirt, I let my hands revel in the feel of his bare skin under my hands. All the while, he takes me. Hard. Fast. Furious. Without the slightest hint of a second thought or a moment of hesitation. He slams in and out, grinding against me, grunting softly from the effort.

I hold him with arms, legs, pulling him deeper, raking my nails down his back and taking wicked pleasure in the way he hisses. His thrusts pick up speed, grow stronger, until our bodies crash together in a strange pain/pleasure mix I've never experienced before now and won't be able to live without after tonight.

He takes me.

I take him.

We both know what we want and we ride each other, using each other for our pleasure, delighting in the pleasure of the other. I want it to last forever but it can't, since we're both already tensing with the onslaught of climax. I clutch him tight, our bodies crushed together as my muscles clamp around his length like a vice. He groans, losing himself in me, trembling as he comes.

My head's in a whirl, my thoughts circling around so fast it's enough to make my brain ache.

Oh, my God. What did we just do? The only sounds in the room are that of us catching our breath. I've never let myself go like that before, and the stakes have never been so high. My boss. No, not just my boss—the CEO of the company. Damn…the owner of the company.

Whom I hate.

I hate him, right?

I did. At least, I thought I did. There's a thin line. I've never truly understood the truth of that statement until now. The line between love and hate is indeed, thin. Not that I love him. Nowhere near it. But there's been an insane undercurrent of attraction running through my resentment of him since the night we had our fight. And he clearly feels the same, or else we wouldn't have just gone at it like a pair of horny rabbits, right here in the middle of the lab.

He's still on top of me, still breathing like a wild animal, and I can't bring myself to let him go. But I have to. I need to. I can't forget why I'm here or what it means for me to be part of this project. It was the frenzy of the moment, is all. The tension we've both been dealing with for so long, the relief, and finally that rush at our success. It all came out like this and that's that.

And that is all there is to it.

A simple explanation for a terrible mistake.

So…why can't I let him go?

LINCOLN

W hy the hell can't I let her go?

I can't control anything about myself where she is concerned, evidently. But I don't want to move. I don't want anything to destroy this moment, because I know nothing will be the same after this. People say all the time that sex doesn't have to change anything, but that's horseshit. Sex on an office floor changes everything.

A floor might make an exciting alternative to a big comfortable bed when it comes to sex, but it's damn well nowhere to linger afterward, when there's a sexy body crushed underneath you. I roll over to give her air.

Her face is flushed, her eyes bright as she stares up at the ceiling with a look of—what? Amazement? I'd like to think so, but it's probably more like disbelief that she landed underneath me, or acute embarrassment. I can imagine the thoughts running through her head. What happens now that the heat of the moment has passed? Has she fucked up her career? And the famous female preoccupation...will he still respect me professionally.

Bottom line, deep down—I don't give a damn about any of it.

She got under my skin from the moment Ryland moved to one side and she came into view. Hell, I already want her again. She's a tempting devil, and everything I've been missing—beauty, brilliance, passion. I knew there was a volcano under all that snow, just waiting to erupt. I'm just glad I was here when it did.

Her body is a thing to be worshipped, just as I had imagined when I jacked off to a fantasy about her in shower. Her breasts are full and heavy, the sort a boy dreams about when he's young and just figuring out the differences between himself and the girl next door. Her stomach is slim, with that lovely soft swell. A man wants a little softness—at least, I do. And curvy hips, perfect to hold onto as I drive myself into her unbelievably tight pussy. My cock starts to stir again, just thinking about it.

She sits up, still flushed. "Your mother would be ashamed of you."

I laugh softly. And there I was worried about her being embarrassed. I know I want more of her.

Much more.

I open my mouth to answer her, but it's not the sound of my voice that floats into the room, but Maddie's.

"Daddy?" my daughter cries out.

I freeze as her voice is followed by the sound of soft weeping. "Oh, shit," I mutter under my breath. "Hey, honey. Be right there. Just wait for me." I button my shirt as fast as I can.

"Do you think we woke her?" Sam whispers, horrified, as she hooks her bra and holds her blouse closed.

"I doubt it. She would've woken up during, if we had," I point out, hoping to God I'm right. I lift my hips to fasten my pants. Talk about scarring a kid for life. Waking up to find her father pile driving one of his employees. Fuck, my mother *would* be ashamed of me. I scramble to my feet and once I'm certain I'm presentable, I hurry over to her.

She's just sitting up, rubbing her eyes. I let out a sigh of relief when I note the position of her blankets and pillow. She hasn't moved out of her makeshift bed. "What is it, sweetheart?"

"Where am I?" she mumbles.

"You're at my lab."

"Oh. I thought Mommy had come and taken me to Juan's house."

"I'm sorry, honey." I sit cross-legged, close to her. "You were asleep, and I wanted to come down to the lab so I brought you with me."

"It's okay, Daddy. I got scared when I woke up and I couldn't see you," she mutters. Her eyes are still a little bleary from sleep and crying.

I feel like the world's worst father. Something tells me I'm going to make big changes in my life. I don't want to feel guilty again. "I'm sorry," I repeat gently, wishing there was something else to say. "I think it's about time for us to get home, anyway. You can sleep in your bed now."

"That's nice," she says, then yawns wide to enough to split open her head. It's enough to make me yawn, too, and we both chuckle.

Sam clears her throat behind us.

Maddie cranes her neck to get a look at the newcomer.

"Hi," Sam whispers.

I look at her over my shoulder and find that she's wiggling her fingers in a little wave.

"Hi," Maddie whispers back, waving and looking a little awed. "Who are you?"

"I'm Sam. I work with your dad." By now, she has put herself back together and is clearly better at things like this than I am. She's being warm and sweet.

Maddie seems to quickly pick up on this. "You work with my daddy?" she asks, her eyes curious.

"I do."

"Are you a whore?"

Both Sam and I jerk back in surprise. "Maddie, why did you say that?" I ask with a frown.

Maddie looks at me innocently. "Mommy said all the women who work with you are whores."

My blood starts to boil, but when I glance at Sam, she trying her best not to laugh. I turn back to Maddie and smile tightly. "I think your mother was joking when she said that.

To start with I don't work with … whores and I don't think you should be using that word either."

"Why not?"

"Because it's rude."

"Oh." She nods then turns to Sam. "What *do* you do?"

"I'm an engineer." Sam walks forward and sinks to her knees on the blankets, hands clasped in her lap. "See, we're working on this new piece of equipment—"

"The pro…to…type," Maddie interjects, enunciating carefully.

"That's right." Sam beams. "And it's my job to make sure it works right. There are so many little pieces and it's so important for every little piece to work well together, because if just one little thing isn't working the way it's supposed to…"

"Kablooey," Maddie shouts, spreading her hands in an explosive gesture.

"Maybe not quite so dramatic." Sam grins. "But I think you get the picture. We made a lot of progress tonight, and things are going to go much more smoothly for your daddy and you from now on."

My daughter looks to me, hopeful. "Isn't that good, Daddy?"

"Yes, that's very good," I agree. There's so much more to it than this—Sam doesn't know about the leaks in the company, the fact that Weissman is using our technology to further his little empire—but for now, it's enough. That reminds me. "I wouldn't write up any reports about what just happened yet," I muse, trying to sound casual.

"Why not?" she asks, frowning, immediately forgetting Maddie's presence.

"Let's just keep it between ourselves," I advise. "We want to be sure we can replicate the test's success, and then test how long the prototype can stay airborne on the same battery. We want to run altitude tests, too. We're not quite out of the woods yet." It's all a ruse, of course. I'm more certain than ever that we hit on the right combination of tweaks, but if there's still an active leak in the company... Weissman should never find out.

She doesn't understand. A cloud drifts over her face. Maybe she thinks I don't want to give her credit or something. Still, she nods. "All right. I'll keep it confidential."

"You'll get the credit you deserve, of course."

She frowns, and the cloud thickens. "I wasn't even thinking about that."

"Well. Just in case you were."

"I wasn't. Is that all you think I care about?" she lashes out.

I'm about to open my mouth and let a lot of stupid things pour out, but thank God for the presence of my daughter. She doesn't need to hear such things. She's my saving grace right now. I manage to maintain my cool, flashing a tight smile. How did things shift so quickly? "No. It isn't. I only wanted to ease your mind. Of course, I won't forget what an important contribution you've made here. Your work has been more than appreciated."

Her eyes widen for a brief moment, and color floods her cheeks.

For fuck's sake, that was clumsy, too. It sounds like I was making a comment about what we just did on the floor. I can't talk about it in front of the kid. I shouldn't have said anything. Why does she turn me into a bumbling idiot every time? I'm the CEO of this company, for Christ's sake. I command respect. I'm on top of everything in my life. I'm even making headway with my kid. But dealing with her? I put my foot in my mouth every single time

"I should go," she says, standing abruptly.

"Are you mad with me because I said the rude word?" Maddie asks, innocent and oblivious. Lucky her.

"No, of course not, sweetie." Sam smiles. "It's just awfully late, and I have to get home and go to sleep."

"You're sure you'll be all right getting there? Let me call you a cab," I offer.

The look she gives me could pulverize stone. "Thank you, but that won't be necessary. I'm used to working late and driving home afterwards." She turns to Maddie, smiling again. "I'm so glad to meet you, Maddie."

"Bye, bye, Sam. I'll see you tomorrow!"

There's enough hope in her voice to tear my heart. The last thing she needs to do is form an attachment to my employee. It's bad enough I did.

When we're alone again, with me cursing my stupidity, Maddie yawns again. "Can we go home now, Daddy?"

"Sure thing," I reply, acting on autopilot as I gather the blankets and pillow. She makes a funny picture, standing there in a pair of Minnie Mouse pajamas and bare feet, brown curls standing out in all directions like corkscrews—dammit. I still need to learn how to braid her hair— all while holding a teddy bear by its arm. Definitely not what anyone would expect to see in a tech lab.

A lot of things have happened tonight that no one would expect to see in a sophisticated lab like this one. I turn my head to look at the video camera. We usually turn it on to record every flight, but thank God, we didn't switch it on. I wouldn't want to run the risk of the network getting hacked and leaving ourselves open to having our progress monitored.

"Come on, honey." I pick her up and rest her on my hip. She leans a sleepy head on my chest as I turn off the lights. I can't shake the thought that I'm losing something important as I walk out into the hallway and hear the lock click behind me. My daughter's head bounces gently on my shoulder as I walk to the elevator.

"I'm glad it's the weekend now," Maddie whispers as we walk.

"How come?"

"It means I'll have you all to myself."

LINCOLN

Maddie and I are nearly finished with painting her room. The last of her chicken pox spots have cleared from her skin and now that she's at a hundred percent, the kid is like a whirling dervish. A whirling dervish with a mouth that never stops moving. I swear she hasn't stopped speaking since she woke up yesterday morning.

Who'd have thought after living on my own all these years and grown set in my ways, I could bear to have a non-stop chatter box. In my apartment. For the whole weekend. With no office distractions. Just the two of us. Where I can't even hear myself think.

But in fact, having Maddie around is like a breath of clean fresh air. She turns my apartment from the lifeless, cold, stone and steel contraption into a place of laughter and life. Now when I think about it, it's a damn disgrace, the way this penthouse has sat virtually unused ever since I bought it after the divorce went through. I'd been living in hotels after moving out of the house I shared with Regina and Maddie out of a sense of hope. Maybe I'd win custody and need a house.

Now I have her back and her innocent talk, far from being irritating or bothersome, is a sweet distraction from the unwelcome direction my thoughts seem to keep moving in. Yeah, those thoughts are called Samantha Harper. I need Ms. Harper running around inside my brain like I need a hole in my head.

I'm not in love with Sam or anything, but I have it bad for her. I wish I wasn't so damn obsessed with her. She's the only woman who has ever been able to get under my skin and stay there. Sure, I wanted Regina, but that felt more like snake poison spreading through my system. I was so naïve and desperate to make it work I simply imagined all the good things I saw in her. Any kindness, warmth, or joy I made up in my head because that was what I wanted to see. I married a figment of my imagination.

Sam is different. More direct. Real. Honest. Genuinely warm. The way Maddie warmed up to her is proof of that. Kids and dogs always know who they're dealing with. She is the opposite of Regina.

The first time I took Regina out for a meal she offered to pay half. Of course, I didn't take her up on her offer, but I was so damn naïve and stupid I was impressed. I didn't see it for what it was. A ploy to make her appear the opposite of what she was... a spoilt rich girl. If Sam offered, it would be because she makes it a point to pay her half of the meal all the damn time!

And I have to grudgingly admit to myself, she's a lot fucking smarter. She was right all along. It was the design that needed tweaking. Just watching her work on that circuit board was like watching a maestro conducting a symphony.

On top of it all, she's a hottie. Her body is hot enough to fry a dozen eggs on. The way we went at it on the lab floor. Like wild animals. It was raw, uncontrollable fiery. She touched something in me that I haven't acknowledged in a long time. I'd previously believed any hope of passion, excitement or a real true connection with a woman had faded away. She proved me wrong.

Somewhere in this city, she is having a great weekend, unaware she has ruined me. Not to mention got me so fucking horny, I'm afraid my daughter will ask me why I've stuffed a whole salami in my trousers. I realize I just need to chill, not fantasize about calling her and asking her what she's wearing. God, I'd love to know though. She has some tits on her. Big. Bouncy. Lush. I keep thinking of her standing in front of me, naked and oiling those marvelous tits. And my cock gliding, slipping, fucking those oily breasts.

The obsession comes back in full force.

Count to ten, dude. Count to fucking ten. You sure as hell are not in the market for any kind of relationship with a woman.

Especially now, since I have Maddie to think about. Bringing a woman into my life would mean bringing her into my daughter's life too, which will mean complications and potentially more painful consequences if things don't work out. I want to concentrate on Maddie. Make up for lost time. Really get to know her.

"Daddy, did you hear what I said?" Maddie demands from the floor.

I carry on running the roller on the wall, but look down at her. She is splattered in a variety of colors. I love this kid to bits. "Uh, no, sorry. Can you repeat the question, please?"

"I said, how old is Sam?"

The roller comes to a stop on the wall. "I don't know. Why?"

"Just wondering," she says and carries on painting the lower half of the wall. "She's very pretty."

I grin to myself. "Who?"

"Sam."

"Yes, I guess she is."

"Do you have a girlfriend, Daddy?"

I glance sideways at her.

She isn't looking at me, but at the spot, she's painting.

"No, I don't. After we paint your room what furniture do you want to put in it?"

"I haven't thought about it yet," she says solemnly.

"How about that rocking chair I bought for your last birthday?"

She stops painting and looks down the tray. "It's okay, Daddy. Don't worry about it. It's too far to bring."

I stare at her. I already know her ways. When she looks down, she's trying to hide something. "Maddie, I can easily get it sent over."

She looks up at me then and exhales heavily. "I don't know where it is."

My eyes are narrowed. "Why not?"

Her eyes slide away. "Mommy gave it away."

I stare at her bent head. "What?"

My six-year old daughter looks me in the eye and states, "Mommy always gives away all the toys you send to me."

I try not to show my rage. *Regina, you vile bitch you.* Whatever did I see in that psychopath I'll never know. I'm starting to really hate her. If she were here, I couldn't guarantee I would be able to stop myself from slapping her conceited, plastic face. I force a smile for Maddie's sake. "It's okay, honey. We'll just have to go out and get you a whole bunch of brand new toys, won't we?"

She beams up at me. "Daddy, can I have that Japanese doll back too? I don't mind not having the Miss Osaka, but I do miss Miss Toyko and her green Kimono."

It's been a long time since I felt choked up with emotion. I didn't even cry at my parents' funeral. I was too shocked by the way they were suddenly both gone. Just like that. Without even a goodbye. Their car hit a speeding grain and silage trailer. The driver was drunk and their bodies were so mangled they had to have closed caskets.

But hearing my daughter ask for the Japanese doll I bought her when she was four makes me want to bawl my eyes out. All these years, I've been sending gifts and that selfish bitch has been quietly and mercilessly getting rid of them. What kind of woman is she?

"Daddy?" Her little forehead is creased and her lips are pursed.

"Yes?"

"What am I going to do tomorrow when you have to go to work?"

"You'll come to work with me again, but Tuesday is Fourth of July, so I'll have that day off, and we can go to the fair a few blocks over, if you want to. They'll have fireworks and things like that. You think you might want to do that?"

She nods vigorously, curls bouncing everywhere. "Yes," she gushes. "That will be sooooo fun!"

"But there's something else we have to do first. Tomorrow night after I finish work, we're going to meet with a few potential nannies. We'll leave early. Does that sound good?"

She hangs her head. "I guess…"

I crouch down next to her. "What's the matter?"

"It's just that…" She sighs. "I already had so many nannies. I'm sorta tired of them."

"Oh honey, I'm sorry about that." I put an arm around her small shoulders. "You can't come to work with me every day. Little girls are not supposed to do that, but it won't be like it was when you were living in England. I promise."

"You don't know what it was like there, though," she points out, ever reasonable.

I smile. "True. You can tell me about it, you know."

"I know." She sighs, a child with the weight of the world on her shoulders.

I want to take that weight away from her. She's too young for it. "Well. How about you tell me when you're ready," I say when she remains silent. I won't push her. I want her to feel she can trust me. That means knowing when it's time to press and when it's time to step back and give her space to come to me on her own.

I don't doubt that any nanny Regina left in charge of her daughter was thoroughly vetted. It doesn't sound as though this is a case of mistreatment. Aside from the chicken pox, she seems to be a normal, healthy little girl. Wise beyond her years, certainly. Lonely, but not abused.

"What if I kept coming to your office, but I stayed with Sam during the day?" she suggests.

I manage to cringe only on the inside at the mention of Sam's name. "I don't think that would work, baby."

"Why not?"

"Because Sam has work to do."

"So do you and I stayed in your office," she points out.

"Yes, but I moved a lot of things around for your sake this past week. Not that I wasn't happy to do it," I add quickly. "But Sam can't do that. She's working on the prototype, remember? We have to get it finished by the time the conference comes."

She nods slowly. "Will I get to see her again, do you think?"

"You really like her, huh?"

"Yeah. She's nice. And pretty."

"She is both those things," I agree.

"Is she's smart?"

"Yes, she's very smart, too."

"Do you think I'm smart enough to be an engineer someday?"

"Of course, you are, but I'll be proud of you, no matter what you decide to become."

She seems content with this. "Do you think Sam likes ice cream, Daddy?"

"What?" I ask, fists clenched outside her line of sight.

Her head pops up, a big grin on her face. "Maybe, when she isn't busy, she can come over and have ice cream with us. What do you think?"

Sam, Sam, Sam. No matter how I try, I can't get away from her. It would seem she's cast her spell over my daughter, too.

LINCOLN

I wake up a wreck after spending a sleepless night. All I did was toss, turn and finally, out of desperation, jerk off, but the yearning for her body is so intense not even that would relieve the ache. Now that I've had a taste of her sweetness, I want more. She lit a fire in me that I can't extinguish.

I'm irritable by the time we arrive at the office.

Maddie knows the drill, setting herself up in a corner of my office and settling in to play with her tablet and coloring books. The building is virtually empty, thanks to it being the Fourth tomorrow. Most of my staff people have turned it into a four-day weekend. If I had to take a guess, I'd say Sam didn't.

The need to chase her is incredible. Like some prehistoric caveman hunter, I feel my body hum, as if I am near prey or a source of water. The tension is nearly unbearable. I want to go to her. Right this minute. I want to throw her down on that metal table in the lab and slam into her. Hard. All day long.

"Daddy?"

"Yeah, honey."

"Do you think Sam came to work today?"

"Maybe," I mutter distractedly. Truth is, I know shit about her. I'm her boss. It's perfectly within my rights as the company CEO to access the HR files and take a look.

It's shocking how truly un-disappointed in myself I am for stooping this low. Her picture pops up on my screen. I enlarge it. Even in this photo, her hair is tightly held back and there is only a ghost of a smile on her face. My eyes scan her bio. So she lives in a rather modest part of town. As a senior engineer, she could easily afford something better. She could be supporting a relative or paying off some massive debt. College maybe?

Unmarried. I knew that already. But her file doesn't provide much more insight into her private life. No mention of a significant other. She wouldn't have fucked me if she had a boyfriend, would she? Doesn't seem the type, but women are a mysterious bunch. I can't make the same mistakes I did before. I can't fool myself into believing she's someone she isn't.

Maybe she's with him right now. Maybe he's touching her, kissing her. Just the mere thought of her being with another man makes my heart pound fast and my temper flare. My head feels hot and tight. I can't think straight with the blood rushing in my ears. She's mine. I have to make her mine.

"Can you entertain yourself up here for a little while?" I ask, turning to Maddie.

She nods.

"If you need anything just pick up that phone and call Erica or me, okay?"

"Okay, Daddy." Maddie agrees with a nod.

I head straight out to the elevator. I have to see her. I need to be with her. To touch her skin. I need to know she knows what Friday night meant to me. And how much I hate the awkward way we left things.

When I open the door, swinging it to the side, I find that she's not alone.

"What do you mean, you don't have any plans?" Ryland teases.

Is he fucking flirting with her? My blood pressure shoots up.

"You're too young and pretty not to have something to do during the holiday," he adds.

Yes, he is definitely flirting with her.

"I'm a workaholic. Sue me," she says, grinning...until she spots me filling up the doorway, and glowering down at the two of them. "Oh. Good morning." There's nothing on her face, in her eyes, or tone of voice, to give the impression that anything ever happened between us.

What transpired three nights ago, may as well have been a dream. Something I imagined.

"Hey, Big Boss. Good morning. How was your weekend?" Ryland asks, completely oblivious.

"It was fine," I reply, never looking away from her.

She's blank-faced. Polite, professional, but nothing more.

I can't talk to her with him around. I can't very well kick him out of the room when the prototype which was used in testing, is sitting alongside the one we plan to use during the demonstration. They clearly plan to apply her solution to the new prototype and run a test.

Ryland gives me a strange look. "Everything okay?"

How can I possibly feel like an outsider in my own lab? It's all too ridiculous. I won't let her make a fool out of me. "Yeah, everything is just fine. I'll leave the two of you to your work," I say casually, backing out of the room.

"Don't you want to hear what Sam came up with?" Ryland asks, his eyes glowing with excitement.

I shake my head and before anybody realizes I'm a jealous lunatic, I step out into the corridor. "No. Surprise me when it's done."

SAMANTHA

As soon as his footsteps die away, I deflate like a dammed balloon. I lower my gaze to the drone, my mind whirling.

He looked like a man in a fever when he stepped into the lab. I wonder if he knows it. I wonder if Ryland noticed. They know each other so well he would have been bound to pick up on something strange from his best friend.

Or maybe, I'm just kidding myself. Maybe I'm mistaking embarrassment for some deeper emotion. He must have come to tell me to forget what we did on the floor. Pretend it never really happened. He doesn't need to. The sane part of me would have to agree with him. It was such a colossal mistake. I don't know what I was thinking. I've never behaved in such a wanton way ever. I have to stop thinking about him.

That's *all* I did *all* weekend, and where did it get me? Nowhere.

RIVER LAURENT

"Everything all right between you two?" Ryland asks, scratching his jaw.

"Mmmm…"

"You didn't have another fight when I wasn't around, did you?"

"No, no," I reply, telling the truth for once. "No, it's just… awkward. As always. I guess it always will be. He doesn't like me."

"Eh, I think you're wrong," he jibes, winking. "He's just a stubborn son of a bitch when he wants to be. That's all. He hates to admit when he's been acting like a dick."

I wince at his choice of word. It was my word, but now I feel disloyal for letting Ryland say that about Lincoln. He's not a dick. And even if he is a dick, he's my dick. The thought brings me up short. *What the hell am I doing?*

"Anyway, don't let him get to you. Just keep plugging away." Ryland stands, pushing his stool back. "I have to get back to my office and wrap up a few things. I'd like to make it an early day."

"Understood. Enjoy the holiday." I wish I felt even a fraction of the enthusiasm in my voice. I feel nothing but—empty. Disappointed and confused by the way I can't get my thoughts straight when it comes to Lincoln.

Ryland leaves and I sink down in a chair. I stare at the drone blankly. It's useless, trying to get any work done right now. This isn't like me. Work has always come first. And this work is far too important to let something like my hormones get in the way.

I pull the clip from my hair and shake it out of its bun, sighing. I wish we hadn't done it. I wish we could do it again. Back and forth, back and forth, like a ping pong ball. For two solid days, that's what I put myself through.

I keep cursing myself for letting the adrenaline rush of solving the overheating issue go to my head.

Longing for him.

Wondering whether it'll make things even more uncomfortable between us.

Wishing I could be with him again—alone, this time, without the chance of being caught.

Wishing I had never seen him in the first place.

No, no, no. I stop just short of pushing the prototype from the table—no sense losing my job—and wonder why I bothered coming in today. Maybe because I needed to see him. Or because I needed to be in the room where it happened.

I look down at the spot where we made love, right there on the floor. Lovemaking isn't what it was. It was primal, wild, uncontrollable, dirty, hot, unbelievable. Like nothing that has ever happened to me.

What am I, nuts? I'm going to have to look at that spot every day for the duration of my job here. Why would I put myself through that? The constant, daily reminder of how stupid I was. Because no matter how good it felt, it's now finished, the moment is over, and it's left me a hot mess. It was stupid, end of story.

I've wanted a lot of things in my life. Who hasn't? And I've managed to work my way into a few of them, including this job. But there were many things I didn't get, too. I learned to live with that, the way anybody else does. I'll have to learn to live without him, no matter how much I want him.

It's all in the past now. There's no reason for me to fall under a spell like that, ever again. Because it was just adrenaline. Relief. Shared happiness over breaking through a major setback.

That's all.

No, it isn't, a voice in my head whispers. I stare at the floor again. In my heart, I know that's not all, not by a long shot. If there were nothing between us to begin with, we wouldn't have ended up wrapped in each other. Immediately, like we were magnetized, we flew to each other. It felt so right and when he was inside me, I felt as if he belonged there, even though he stretched me the way no man has, and it actually hurt being filled like that. But when it was over and he pulled out, it wasn't relief I felt. I actually felt it like a loss. My body cried for him.

That's not the sort of thing that just happens. Passionate, frenzied, incredibly satisfying sex with a man like him— doesn't just happen unless there's an undercurrent of something else beneath it.

I know what that undercurrent is.

I was right to act cool and professional with him earlier, I decide as I gather my things. I presented the solution to Ryland and that's all I had to do today. Thanks to our breakthrough on Friday, I don't have to be here. I don't even know why I came and staying here any longer is nothing more than torture at this point. A day off tomorrow will help clear my head a little more.

Yeah, right. I roll my eyes. Because an entire weekend did that so well.

I test the lock to be sure it's secure and start walking down the empty corridor. For the first time in my adult life, I wish I weren't such a workaholic. It would be nice to have something to do tomorrow, the way people my age generally do. Some sort of diversion.

I've always dismissed that sort of thing in favor of proving myself at school or in the lab. Look where it's gotten me. The one place I've always felt secure, always felt like I could contribute and prove myself worthy, is the one place where I now feel like I can't be without wanting to tear my boss' clothes off.

Or tear my heart out.

LINCOLN

"I wanna go over there! No, wait, over there! Oh, Daddy, can I have cotton candy?" My daughter's eyes shine with the sort of frantic light only sensory overload can provide.

I had no idea the fair would be anything like this. The street is completely clogged with people and their exuberant energy. I've heard it is amazing, which was why I wanted to bring Maddie here, but I might have reconsidered if I'd known it was going to be this frenetic.

No, I wouldn't have.

Not when I see how overjoyed she is.

The day is hot and humid as it made Maddie's already curly hair nearly stand on end. She looks so funny as she swivels her head back and forth in an attempt to take in the clowns, jugglers, face painters. Musicians, dancers, street artists. And the food, so many competing smells I can hardly tell one from the other. Sweet, salty and oily have all come together to create the sort of perfume one can only ever smell at an event such as this.

A little girl with pigtails passes in front of us and I suddenly realize that I need a woman in my life to show me how to do a little girl's hair. Maybe Liz, our new nanny, can give me a few pointers. Lord knows there's nobody else to ask.

Not...

Nope. I can't think about her. Today is Daddy time with Maddie. Besides, I didn't like the way I felt when I saw Sam with Ryland. I knew there was nothing going on between them, but I wanted to knock his head off his neck so bad, my teeth ached. I never felt that way about any woman before Sam. It is a bad sign. Also, it pissed me off when Sam looked at me yesterday as though I had imagined our last encounter when she had fucked me as if she was starving for it. I hate women who run hot and cold. I don't need complications in my life.

Maddie tugs at my hand. I look down at her. "Can I have cotton candy?" she reminds me.

"You can, but only if you eat something real first," I say decisively. I have learned that I need to be firm with Maddie. On Saturday, she somehow managed to manipulate me into letting her eat Nutella for breakfast, lunch, and dinner. When I think back now, I don't know how exactly she did it, but I'm wiser now. A lot wiser. We won't ever be having a repeat of that. When she next comes up with another gem like ketchup is a vegetable, I'll know exactly what to say.

"You mean like a funnel cake?" she asks innocently.

See what I mean about this kid. I frown.

Now she starts laughing, her eyes sparkling brighter than ever. It seems as though she's been skipping ever since we arrived, the light sundress Erica gave her as a present swishing around her knobby, little girl knees.

I've had to hold back the urge to tell her to stop, to watch where she's going even though I've kept a tight grip on her hand since the moment we stepped outside. I don't want her to trip and skin her knees, but I don't want to tamp down that exuberance, either. I'm beginning to recognize the fine line a parent has to walk. "No, not funnel cake. How about a hamburger?" I suggest since I don't think the chances of finding anything healthier here are very high.

"C'mon, Daddy, please. It's a holiday!"

I gaze at her adorable face.

"Please, Daddy."

Poor thing had to live with Regina for the last two years. Oh, what the hell? She's right. I should loosen up a little. Just this one last time. "Fine," I say sternly. "But no more sweets after that until you've had dinner. And that's non-negotiable."

My daughter is a smart cookie and knows when she's won, so she readily agrees and gives my legs a quick hug. Then she finishes a ball of cotton candy bigger than her head while we walk through the throng of people.

Afterwards, we find a stand selling fresh-grilled burgers and hot dogs. I normally favor a very healthy diet, but my mouth floods with saliva when the scent of grilled meat hits my nose.

Minutes later, we're sitting on a random stretch of curb with our burgers, watching the world go by. She has so many questions. I barely remember the days of my childhood, when everything was so fresh and new. When life was only just beginning to make an impression on me. And it's funny, but she helps me see things through those eyes again. I feel younger when I'm with her. Less jaded.

"Why does that man look so unhappy?" she asks, jerking her chin in the direction of a dour old man whose mouth is set in a deep frown. His brows are drawn together as he elbows his way down the sidewalk. He's dressed sloppily, or maybe it's the sweat rolling off his forehead and soaking into his t-shirt that gives that impression.

Normally, I would ignore him, or at most mutter something in his general direction if he were to bump into me. Now, with my daughter seated beside me, I look at him. I really look at him. "He's probably lonely," I decide. "Tired… sad… and hot. Old. He doesn't have anybody to enjoy the day with him. Maybe he doesn't like crowds."

"He lives in a big city, though," she reasons before taking a bite from her burger, leaving ketchup at the corners of her mouth.

"That's true. I guess he should be used to it. Some people are so grumpy, though, that they don't notice all the good things around them. All they see is what makes them unhappy."

She thinks about this, chewing slowly as she does. I can almost see the wheels turning. "That's a shame. I wish I could do something to make him happier."

I kiss the top of her sun-warmed head. "I know you do, but it's important to remember that you can't make everybody happy. You know? Some people are just plain old unhappy and you have to leave it at that. Don't take it personally. It doesn't have anything to do with you."

"Daddy, can I give him my burger?"

I stare at her. "Why do you want to do that?"

"Because he's hungry and I'm not," she says simply.

For a second, I am stunned by the humanity in my daughter. Then I feel shame flood through me. That thought never even crossed my mind. I grasp her hand and stand up. "Come on."

We walk up to the man. "Hello."

His body shrinks and he looks at me with an expression that is almost fear. Maybe, all he knows is people who want to move him on or hurt him. I open my wallet, pull out all the bills in it and thrust it into his hands. "Go buy yourself some lunch."

He looks shocked. "You don't have to give me this much," he says in a trembling voice.

"It's not from me. It's from my daughter."

He looks at down at Maddie. She grins at him and his eyes fill with tears. "God, bless you, child. God bless you," he mutters. He reaches out a hand and touches her head, but his hands are so filthy I feel a sudden flare of alarm and the protective instinct that only Maddie manages to inspire in me, takes over. I pick my daughter up and seat her on my shoulders. "Good luck," I say to the man and walk away. I look up and Maddie is waving to the man she just helped.

"Look, Daddy, there's a lady holding two ice cream cones in her hands," she cries from high above my head.

"Good for her," I say, navigating my way through the crowd

"Now I want ice cream," she says.

I shake my head at the audacity of my kid. "I thought we agreed no more sweets until after dinner now."

"But when I saw the ice cream..." she trails off, following the progress of the double-fisting woman with great interest.

I barely stifle a smile as I scan the immediate area in search of the ice cream stand. Just for today.

"Daddy! Daddy, quick put me down," Maddie says, squirming on my shoulder.

"What?" I ask, lowering her to the ground. The next thing I know, I'm being led through the crowd, zigging and zagging in between clusters of people.

"Slow down! What's the emergency?" Then, I almost slam straight into the emergency, which isn't an emergency at all. It's a petite, curvy, blonde woman with familiar eyes and cheeks that flush the instant she recognizes me.

"What are you doing here?" I manage to choke out, only inches from Sam.

She looks gorgeous in a thin-strapped dress and sandals, her hair in a bun at the back of her head. She looks soft and feminine, a contrast from her professional attire.

She frowns slightly, eyes moving this way and that as if she's searching for an escape route. "Uh, I live in the city," she mumbles. "And I didn't have any other plans, so..."

"Are you here alone?" I can't help but ask. She better not say she's here on a date because I would relish the feeling of my fist against his jaw.

"Yes," she blurts out, still looking for all the world like a deer in headlights.

I'm absolutely the last person she wants to see right now, that much is obvious. But she's hooked too, and there's no escape. I know how tight my daughter's grip is, and she's now grasping Sam's hand with both of hers.

"Hi, Sam!" she beams, nearly bouncing up and down in her excitement.

Sam smiles down at my daughter her tension dissolving somewhat. "Hi, pretty girl. I love your dress. Are you having fun today?"

"Yes, Daddy and I have been having sooooo much fun! We saw jugglers and a man who ate fire! He ate real fire! Did you see him?"

"No, I didn't." Sam chuckles, shaking her head.

"Daddy says it doesn't hurt him."

The two of them giggle together and I wish she didn't touch my heart the way she does. Something tells me that she doesn't want anything to do with me outside the office—and she would've bolted just now—had Maddie not grabbed her before she had the chance. Dammit, she shouldn't get along so well with my little girl. All she's doing is making it impossible to forget her.

"Why don't you come along with us?" I suggest, giving the pair of them an easy smile. "We were on our way to get some ice cream and there's another two blocks we haven't even checked out yet."

Maddie bounces harder than ever, practically bursting with excitement, still holding Sam's hand. "Please? I never had so much fun in my whole life!"

"Not ever?" Sam asks, a frown briefly touching her face as she considers this. She's probably wondering how dull and joyless Maddie's life has been up to this point.

"No! I never went to a fair before. This is one of our fun things, right, Daddy?"

I nod. "We made a list of all the things she wants to do, and this was one of them." Inspiration hits like a bolt from the blue. "I bet it would be even more fun if you walked around with us."

Her brows lower until I can barely make out her eyes. She's pissed off at my blatant use of Maddie as a ploy to get her to come along with us.

I grin and shrug. So bite me!

"Can you come with us, Sam?" Maddie screams.

She heaves a big sigh, then she turns to my daughter and gives her the biggest smile. It's warm enough to melt the ice caps. "All right, then," she says. "Let's see what flavors they have at the ice cream stand. What's your favorite flavor?"

"Chocolate!" Maddie proudly announces, taking one of my hands with the one she's not using to hold Sam firmly in place. She beams up at me, then stage whispers, "See? I told you she should have ice cream with us!"

LINCOLN

"The keys are in my pocket," I whisper as we reach the door to the apartment. At any other time, the sensation of Sam's fingers fishing around inside my khakis would lead to something even more interesting, but the dead weight of a sleeping six-year-old in my arms is like a bucket of, well I wouldn't go so far to say, cold water, because nothing is cold when Sam is around.

Sam balances the massive stuffed elephant I won for her in one arm and unlocks the door.

I catch a glimpse of her eyes while they sweep over the apartment as we walk through.

Maddie stirs, but remains fast asleep as I carry her in. It's been a long day. Though the sun isn't even halfway set, I'm sure she'll sleep through the night.

"Do you need help?" Sam whispers.

"Sure, thanks." I carry my daughter to the bathroom, where I sit her on the vanity beside the sink. She lifts her head, but barely, and Sam seems to understand what to do without being asked. She wets a washcloth and runs it over Maddie's face, wiping away the last remnants of ice cream and another head-sized cotton candy she still, somehow, managed to convince me to buy for her. The kid is like a hypnotist. Before I knew it, I was handing over the money and she was holding another cloud of spun sugar.

Without hesitating, Sam also removes Maddie's sandals and washes her dust-streaked feet. I hate to admit to myself that I wouldn't have thought of it, as much as it clearly needed to be done. There are still so many things I don't know, and don't know that I don't know. Years of practice, I've missed out on. I wonder how this comes so naturally to her.

It would feel so right, doing this with her all the time. The two of us taking care of my daughter, working as a team.

I carry Maddie to the spare guest bedroom. Her room is still a work in progress and it still smells of paint. We sit on the bed with me propping Maddie up while Sam gently and quickly changes her into a nightgown. We don't exchange a word, merely pointing and nodding to communicate. Not that it matters. Something tells me a sixty-piece brass band could parade through the apartment and my kid wouldn't budge.

But there's a certain solemnity and closeness in the way we're working together. We're on the same wavelength, acting as two parts of a whole. The way a couple who's been together for years might work as a team while putting their child to bed after a long, exciting day. Both of us are tired, too. Maddie ran us ragged. We exchange a small smile before I tuck her in and plant a kiss on her forehead. The sort of secret smile adults exchange when a child they both care about is happy. As if Maddie doesn't belong to Regina and I, but Sam and I.

I know Sam does care for Maddie. She was endlessly energetic today, allowing herself to be dragged from one place to another without so much as a word of protest.

"You were good to her today," I murmur as we walk up to the kitchen.

"It was easy. She's adorable." Sam shrugs and leans against the counter.

"Something to drink?" I ask, bending in front of the fridge. Anything to keep her around a little while longer. We managed to spend a perfect afternoon together. Not a word about work, or us, or anything that might cause the bubble around us to burst.

"Water, please. It's so hot out there."

"You held up like a champ," I tell her, grinning as I hand over the bottle.

Our fingers brush together and she looks down, a blush coloring her cheeks.

I'll do anything to hold her here, with me, in this moment.

"So did you."

"You made her happy," I murmur, all pretense of flirting or messing around put aside. "Thank you for that. You don't know what it means to me."

"How many years since your divorce?"

Even the thought of the divorce makes me grimace. "Two years, but it feels as if she's been away from me for much longer. I guess the two of us are trying to get to know each other. It would be difficult enough under ordinary circumstances, but the way things are at work..."

She nods slowly. "I can't imagine, but you do seem to be handling it well. She's adjusting and seems to like being with you."

"That makes one person, anyway," I mutter, flashing a wry grin.

"Not everybody is as susceptible to your charms, I guess. Some people have taste," she teases.

"Are you casting aspersions on my daughter's taste?" I say with a mock stern expression.

"Not at all. The poor thing has no choice. You don't get to choose your family." She barely holds back a giggle.

It must be the day we've spent together, but there's a freshness to the energy between us. The tension from yesterday is no longer sizzling between us, probably because we've shared a good day. A wonderful day. The sort of day that leaves a person feeling good afterward. Satisfied. With the impression that life is actually pretty good.

"Thanks," I say

"You make her happy," she replies, meeting my gaze with her own frank, unwavering one. "She needs that." She bites her lip while she decides whether to say what is in her mind, then goes ahead and says it, "I don't think she's had a lot of happiness in her life."

I scowl at the reminder. "How can you tell?"

Her shrug speaks volumes, as does the way she looks over

my shoulder at something far away. "I just can. Call it experience."

I study her.

She's wounded. Somebody ignored her when she was young. Maybe that's why she feels such a kinship with Maddie—two similar souls recognizing each other.

"Then you obviously know how to make her happy." I grin, trying to lighten the mood.

"You seem to be doing a pretty go job of making her happy."

"You think so?"

"Yeah. I think she's lucky to have a father like you. Indulgent, patient."

I grin. "It won't kill you spend some adjectives."

She rolls her eyes so hard she could have checked out her own ass. "Okay. Rude, arrogant, overbearing, dominating, bad-tempered—"

I hold up a hand. "Hold up, I was thinking more in the line of sexy, brilliant, smart, funny, honest, unlike anyone you've ever been with."

She licks her lips and my eyes widen. Fuck, she looks so goddamn hot. My cock starts thickening, lengthening out. The air in the room changes and my blood starts pumping.

"You don't need me to tell you those things. You know you are." Her voice is a throaty whisper.

Suddenly, I can't stop myself. I have to taste her sweet, full mouth again. I step forward and grab her waist.

The heat of her body seeps through our clothes and makes me feel almost high. Her chest heaves. "Lincoln," she gasps.

I can feel her body trembling as I swoop down on her mouth. She kisses me back as if she has been waiting a lifetime for my kiss. The little moan of surrender she makes in my mouth is the most arousing thing that has ever happened to me. So fucking arousing, I'm rock hard for her.

But it gets better.

The kiss deepens, my tongue going in to search for hers, tangling, hooking and pulling it into my own mouth. And sucking the hell out of it. She melts against me. Just as she did in the lab. She's so willing, so ready, so needy. I want to fulfill that need, to meet it with my own and satisfy us both. She brings out the animal in me, the part of any man that wants to take, possess, and make a woman pass out in ecstasy because of him. My hands take another tour of her body in its light cotton dress, stroking and fondling her lush curves.

She lets her head fall back with a sigh, giving me room to run my lips over her throat. Her pulse pounds away beneath her smooth skin, giving away her excitement. I'm fairly sure my heart is racing just as fast, maybe faster. How can I help it? She is so goddamn delicious. When she lets out a soft moan, I feel the reverberation against my lips and smile.

Yeah, she's mine.

She gasps when I cup her firm, full ass with both hands, kneading, then lifting her onto the counter. Her legs hook around my hips automatically, drawing me closer to the center of her heat. My entire body stirs with every sigh, every stroke of her long fingers through my hair. She moans into my mouth when I cup her breasts, playing with the

117

round globes as my mouth finds its way down to join my hands in pleasuring her.

"Yes, yes," she whispers, arching her back with her hands flat on the counter to support her.

If there anything sexier than a beautiful woman, her mouth hanging open, lost in sensation, I have never seen it. I'm so hard, I'm fairly sure I'll burst out of my shorts in another minute or two. "I need you," I gasp, grinding against her, sensing her heat through our clothes.

She throws her arms around my neck, whimpering softly as I lower my shorts, then pull her panties to the side. She's so wet, so hot and ready, whispering in my ear, encouraging me, urging me to take her.

I slide in, hard and sure, and she lets out a shaky cry.

"Yes … yes … Sam, yes …" I growl in her ear with every thrust, every time our bodies slam together, her breasts are bouncing in time. She leans back on her hands again, her eyes closed, meeting my thrusts with her own. I take in the sight of her, beautiful and wanton, passionate and hot, clenching ever tighter around my length until she's locked down around me and we're both shuddering in release.

I collapse against her, panting for air, finally lowering my hand from her mouth. She gasps, pressing her mouth to my neck to stifle the little breathless cries coming from her as she recovers. We're both sweaty, the scent of perspiration and sex hangs heavy in the air around us. I haven't had enough. I want to carry her off to the shower and take her all over again with the water beating down on us…

"Oh, my God," she whispers and pushes me away—not hard,

but firmly. Determinedly. "I'm sorry. I don't know what I was thinking. That was just wrong. I'm—I'm just sorry." She slides from the counter, not meeting my eyes and picks up the purse she discarded on the floor when we first arrived.

"You don't have to—"

"Tell Maddie I had a good time today, okay? I'm glad we spent the day together," she mutters, racing for the door.

"Right." Keeping my voice quiet for Maddie's sake while not grabbing her arm and forcing her to stop—is almost a supreme test of my willpower.

"I'll see you at work." She ducks out, being careful to close the door quietly.

The apartment becomes deathly quiet and still. Suddenly—I get it. It is so blindingly clear that I'm surprised it took me this long to realize it.

I thought I just felt unbelievably attracted to this woman, but in fact, she has infiltrated my mind, body, and soul.

SAMANTHA

I stare at my notes, brow knotted. I have to get this solution pinned down and make sure it's all replicable. It's one thing to stumble on the solution in the middle of the night, but another for a production line to get it right every time. So, double and triple checking my work should be my next and only priority.

But first of all I *need* to stop thinking about him …even though I'm working on his drone, which he designed. In his lab, in his building, for his company. Right next to the very spot where we first had sex. And we did it again last night. An image of him standing in his shirt, sleeves rolled up, leaning one hip against the kitchen counter, looking confidently at me. His eyes, his body, his stand, even the air around him vibrated with his power. The man *oozed* power. I think of him, tall, confident as he strode over to me—and what we did afterwards.

What the hell is wrong with me?

I hate dominating, controlling men. God preserve me from

Alphas, no matter how hot they may be. I'd rather die than play the part of barefoot, pregnant wife.

I close my eyes and take a deep breath to center myself, and of course, I fall short. Just as I've been falling short all morning. Every time I hear footsteps outside the door, I'm sure it's him. I'm certain he's about to come in and challenge me as to why I ran out on him last night. The thing is, I don't even know why myself.

Why did I run?

Maybe I was afraid of how much fun I had yesterday with him and Maddie. I had far, far too much fun. The sort of fun a girl could get used to. Feeling like I was part of something. A family. Anyone looking at the three of us as we wandered through the fair, our hands clasped, would've definitely thought we were much more than we are.

The scariest part is realizing it wouldn't bother me at all if somebody mistakes us for a family. I want that. Jesus, I want that.

And then, the sex. The incredible, unbelievable sex. I've never come so hard, so fast, so long. And I've never lost control like that. There's no such thing as control when he's involved, which is terrifying. I've always been able to draw a line, command respect, be the one who says no. Now, I'm spreading my legs before he even asks.

Ugh, he probably thinks I'm a slut. He's my boss. I hate to be one of those women who sleep with their bosses. I always thought I was better than that.

Oh, my God! What would my father say?

"Stop this," I whisper, wiping my sweaty palms on my skirt.

I reach for the prototype and start assembling it according to the plans as I laid them out. I have to approach this as a complete stranger, someone unfamiliar with the work I've slaved over the last couple of weeks. My hands are almost shaking. I take a deep breath and steady them before starting.

Thirty minutes later, the drone is assembled according to my altered plans. I start it up, the way I've done so many times, and monitor the diagnostics as it runs. Just as it did on Friday night, the temperature levels out at temps far lower than they were before. Low enough and for long enough that I'm beyond reasonably certain this solution is replicable.

I clap my hands and whoop, even though I'm all alone in the lab. I'm used to it and I always preferred it this way, though a little part of me wishes Lincoln were here to share in my happiness.

I print off the final dimensions, prouder and more relieved than I've ever felt in my life. Even if I didn't have any feelings for Lincoln, I would have to tell him right away, so it's not wrong for me to scoop up the papers and hurry down the corridor to his office.

I tell myself, it's normal. I'm just excited over scoring a major win and want to smooth things over with him, even just a little. But in my heart I know, I'm just looking for an excuse to see him again. For the time I worked on the drone, I managed to keep him out of my head, but other than that, I can't get him out of my head.

I get the feeling he needs a win, too. And judging from the way he looked at me last night as I just about broke my neck to get out of there, he might not mind knowing there aren't hard feelings between us.

My heart jumps as I hurry up to his office with the printed plans in my hand. I smile politely at Erica.

"Oh good. Drone plans. He'll be happy to see those," she says checking out her mini switchboard before pressing a button and lifting her receiver. "Miss Harper is here to see you." She looks at me and waves me in.

Taking a deep breath, I open the door and close it behind me.

He leans back in his chair, and looks, oh God—delectable. Yesterday, he looked casual and sexy. Today, he's wearing an immaculate dark suit. And he looks edible. I want to unzip him and taste him. Fit my mouth around his cock and suck it.

"What can I do for you?" he drawls, fingers tented under his strong chin.

Ooops, he's in professional CEO mode. "You can congratulate me," I reply.

One eyebrow arches as his eyes trail down my body. "Why's that?" His voice is suddenly pure sex.

It makes the hairs on my hands rise. I ignore the sensation, the coiled tension in the pit of my stomach. I'm quaking on the inside. I want him bad, but I also need him to listen to me, to take me seriously. This is exactly why our being together in a physical way is a terrible idea. I want to be treated as an equal *and* I want to be fucked until I'm sore. "Because," I announce, "I managed to replicate our solution according to the altered plans."

A slow smile starts on his face, distracting me. *Jesus, Sam. Get a hold of yourself.*

I clear my throat and carry on. "I took it step by step from the beginning, like a total newcomer, and made it work just as well as we did over the weekend."

I expected him to be pleased.

I expected him to congratulate me.

I didn't expect him to launch himself from his chair, sweep me up into his arms, lift me high over his head, and twirl me around, as if I weighed no more than Maddie. I'm so taken aback, I can't even catch my breath, let alone ask him to let me go.

Not that I want to. It is the most delicious feeling to be held up by strong arms. The warmth of his hard body and the pressure of his arms as they hold me up feels heavenly.

"You're a little genius, Ms. Harper!" he shouts with a laugh.

Transfixed, I stare down at his laughing face, and then I too, begin to laugh. It is the most amazing feeling in the world to be so in tune with someone. So exactly matched in feeling. The rest of the world stopped existing for us at that moment. It's now just us, taking big gulps of pure joy.

When he sets me on my feet, his strong arms don't unwind from around my waist. "I wish I had champagne in here. I'd pop the cork right now. We need to celebrate."

"And I would accept." I laugh. My knees are weak with a sense of achievement. Or it could be that they're weak because I'm so close to him, and he's so deliriously happy. We both are, but he behaves as if I've actually come in and announced that I've negotiated a stay of execution for him.

His eyes stare deep into mine, our eyes lock. My heart begins to race faster than ever. Our bodies move closer. It an involuntary thing. Completely out of my control. Like magnets. In seconds, our bodies are pressed together tightly. My head is spinning, and I realize I'm breathless.

I couldn't break away from him right now if my life depended on it.

Oh, damn… I'm falling at the first hurdle. Again.

"What did I ever do without you?" he whispers, his breath hot on my face.

Oh, my Lord, I can't breathe. I can't even think. He's doing it to me again, and I like it. I might even love it.

This time, it's me who leans in for a kiss. He catches my face between his warm palms. Then his tongue plunges into my mouth. My knees buckle. He'll have to be strong enough for the both of us, since I simply can't support myself. Not when his tongue is sweeping along the inside of my mouth. Not when he takes my bottom lip between his teeth and bites it before sucking, hard.

I draw in my breath with a sharp gasp, on the thin line between pain and pleasure. But the pain doesn't last long, and the pleasure deepens almost unfathomably. I'm almost excruciatingly aroused already, wetness pooling between my thighs, soaking through my panties as we grope and kiss more frantically with each passing second.

His tongue is like a trail of liquid fire on my neck. He stops at the point where my pulse flutters frantically. "This is your heartbeat, Sam."

I moan helplessly.

He licks the sensitive skin, making me shudder. "God, I can taste how goddamn much you want me," he whispers, as he pulls away and our gazes collide.

Hypnotized by his scent, his touch, his words. I look into his eyes, heavy lidded, and dark with passion. It's just like last night again, only even more forbidden. Beyond that door are people. I didn't lock the door.

"Why did you run away last night?"

I lick my lips. "I don't know."

"Liar," he snarls, and pushes me back, making my butt fall back on the desk.

I look up at him.

He looks dangerous as he stands in front of me, breathing fire.

"You scare me...I want you too much," I whisper.

"Show me how much you want me."

My nerves dance and jump with excitement. "Erica could come in."

"If she did, she'll know to turn around and go right back out."

It's like a light bulb goes on in my head. I'm galvanized into action. Like a crazed woman, I fumble at his belt and fly. Once his pants are at his ankles I lift my hips and allow him to slide my panties down and over my shoes.

Instead of straightening up and plunging into me, the way he did the last two times, he drops to his knees and with a tortured groan, buries that sinfully gorgeous mouth between my thighs. I gasp and close my eyes, completely lost in ecstasy. My head is rolling back and forth, as he laps at my wet folds.

"Fuck, Sam. You taste like a fucking ripe fruit," he growls, as he reaches my aching clit. He teases it with a series of quick strokes that send me over the edge. My thighs clench around his head as I come, shuddering and shaking.

I don't even know where he gets the condom from. My whole body is still quivering from the great rush of pleasure, when I notice him sheathing himself. Without giving me a chance to recover, he thrusts his massive cock straight into me.

"Oh, fuck." I gasp and start building again. My muscles clench tight around him, making every stroke even more blissful. Fire races through me as we take each other hard and fast.

It's over too soon, both of us fighting to keep ourselves silent as we struggle to catch our breath. He leans against me, hands on the desk, and I allow myself to revel in his nearness for another few moments before we become two separate people again.

Why should I bother fighting this? It's all so good, so natural, the two of us falling into each other's arms every chance we get. We're good together. Our chemistry is phenomenal. And as evidenced by the accomplishment we made in the lab, we make a good team.

It's as though we're meant to be.

Why should I keep arguing with myself then, every time we're together? Isn't it easier to accept what's clearly growing between us?

He kisses the side of my throat then my cheek before straightening up and pulling away to fix up his clothes.

I hop off the desk, my knees still a little weak as I pull my panties on. "Do you think Erica heard anything? I did everything I could to be quiet."

"I think we're good. I have soundproofing on the walls."

I've noticed it before, but there was never a reason to mention it. It makes sense, with the conference room adjoining his office. It wouldn't do for sound to filter back and forth.

"We should celebrate," he announces as he slam dunks the used rubber into the small trash can and straightens his tie. His eyes twinkling.

"Didn't we already celebrate, just now?" I whisper.

He chuckles. "I mean an actual celebration. Lunch. A long one. What do you say?"

I freeze, feeling for all the world like a deer in headlights. I want to say yes. The word "yes" is right on the tip of my tongue. I want to prolong whatever is happening between us. And it feels damn good to know we've made such progress. Not to mention the joy of knowing I've made him so happy. But...

"I can't," I whisper, wincing. "I'm sorry. I made plans for lunch today."

A storm cloud rolls through the room, or maybe it only rolls across his face. His eyes go stormy.

Just like that, the moment's over. Like it never happened at all.

"Right." His voice is flinty.

"I'm sorry," I babble, feeling like he's slipping through my fingers. And I had him, too. I had him right in the palm of my hand. And vice versa. If anyone told me a week ago that I'd ever be in a position where I'd want Lincoln the way I do right now, I would've laughed myself sick. Now, I'd do anything to get him back to where we just were a minute ago.

He shrugs and slips his belt thought its hoop. "Hey, it is what it is."

"If I hadn't already said I'd go to lunch, I'd go with you in a heartbeat." I feel small, terribly small, like I'm shrinking by the second.

He's pulling away. Jamming the buttons of his shirt through the holes opposite, almost violently.

I want to explain that it's not what he thinks it is, that I'd rather be with him, but...

My father is waiting to have lunch with me. And it's complicated. I never expected his call, to put it mildly. Not after the scene I made, during dinner on Friday night. I made it plain then that I never wanted to step foot in that house again, and he seemed all right with the idea. He seemed perfectly fine with it, in fact. Maybe a little too fine. Maybe I wanted him to put up a small fight, just enough to show me he cares. I should know better by now.

But then, he called.

It's so unlike him to try to make up for anything he's done, or didn't do. Curiosity got the better of me, I suppose. Even though I wanted to reject him the way he's rejected me so many times before, I couldn't bring myself to do it. I'm still his daughter and he's still my father. However, I'm certain things just don't dissolve so easily. No matter how much we want them to.

"It doesn't matter. It was just a thought," Lincoln mutters, sitting down in front of his computer, his eyes locked on the screen.

Will I ever win with him?

LINCOLN

I can barely keep my anger in check. Not just anger, either. Jealousy. Jealousy so intense, it's almost difficult to breathe properly.

What's happening to me? When did I become this Neanderthal? I don't like feeling this way, as though there's a boa constrictor around my chest while my blood is boiling at the same time. I hear the rushing through my ears as I wish to God she would leave the office and give me back some semblance of privacy.

"Is that all?" I ask, barely managing to keep from snarling, eyes still focused on my screen. I can't look at her. I can't imagine her with another man. It's too much, after what we just did. I can still taste her. I know it's a man. I could tell by the flash of guilt in her eyes. How could she rush off to have lunch with another man after being with me? She sure does get around.

Is that really who she is? Looks like once again, I've deluded myself into seeing qualities in a woman which simply aren't there.

"Lincoln..." She lingers by my door, clearly unwilling to leave things as they are.

I want to tell her to get lost and never come back because damn it, I can't stand who she's turning me into. If this is the way it's going to be, I don't know that even the most explosive sex ever is worth it. "Shouldn't you be on your way to your lunch date?" I ask, cutting her off.

"It's not exactly—"

"For fuck's sake. Can't you take a hint?" I finally look at her and the jealous, petty part of me relishes the look of dismay on her face. "We had fun and I've got to get back to work."

For a second, she looks stricken, as if I just cut her with her knife. Then she lifts her chin. "Sure. Enjoy your work" She opens the door and closes it softly behind her. Still the professional. At least, she can say that for herself.

I, on the other hand, cannot say any such thing. I push away from my desk and pace the floor restlessly.

What hell is wrong with me? Have I completely lost my mind?

I'm behaving like a class one asshole. But what am I supposed to think, when she goes from fucking me on the edge of my desk to telling me she has lunch plans with somebody else? What's so important about her plans that she can't cancel them in favor of lunch with me?

Which is part of the reason I know she's going out with a man. Does she look at him the way she does at me? Does she make him feel like he's the most important person in the world? Does he feel like a king when he's inside her?

"Damn it," I growl, going back to my chair. I sink into it, but shoot up again. I stand and run my hands through my hair. Trying to work is a complete waste of time now. I shouldn't have let it happen. I should've congratulated her for working so hard and let that be the end of it. What is it about her that makes her impossible to resist? Like she's a drug I can't get enough of now that I've gotten a taste.

I run my tongue over my lips, picking up the last lingering bit of her there.

Fuck, how am I supposed to forget her? I don't want to forget her. I don't want to learn to live without ever feeling again, the passion she sparks in me. I didn't know I was capable of anything close to what she does to me. I don't know that I'll ever find a woman who can do the same.

Damn it, indeed. I need to get out of this room. I can't sit here at this desk, minutes after we used it for other things, knowing she's going to meet up with someone else. I can still smell her perfume and the scent we created together.

A short walk around the block should do the trick.

I barrel my way down the hall and into the elevator before anybody can try to pull me aside with their bullshit. I'm already notorious for my short fuse when interrupted with trivialities, but my reaction if anyone should interrupt me right now, would put any prior blow-ups to shame.

When I reach the lobby and step off the elevator, I catch sight of something unexpected—and not entirely welcome. There she is, walking through the revolving doors and out to the sidewalk. Nobody would know that I just fucked her on my office desk less than fifteen minutes ago. She looks absolutely calm and put together.

I hate myself for this, but I need to know. I start to follow her. I need to be sure of who she's meeting up with. If it's a man, I want to know who the man is. I want to be able to size him up and understand whom I'm truly up against. And if it is a girlfriend, or her mother or something, I'll feel like the world's biggest jackass, but I'll also be the happiest jackass in the universe.

She's on the sidewalk now, looking both ways.

Is he late? Standing her up, maybe? Does she feel her heart sinking, the way mine sank when she turned me down for lunch? God, if I were to meet me on the street right now, I'd look at myself with nothing but pity. Maybe a little contempt, come to think of it. I've never followed a woman before. I've never acted like a stalker. Yet, here I am, practically sneaking up behind her.

A long, sleek, black car pulls up fairly close to where she's waiting, and the rear door opens. A man climbs out.

I snarl, my lip curling in disgust. And that's before I recognize who it is. When I do, the blood that was just moments ago racing like fire through my veins turns to ice.

Vince Weissman. That bastard.

How dare he even step foot in front of my building?

He ushers her into his car and follows her, casting a hasty look behind him before closing the door. The car speeds off to wherever the two of them are going.

While I stand here, reeling.

Sam? Having lunch with the CEO of Arcane Technologies? It doesn't make any sense. Why would she be going out with him? Especially after…

The truth hits me like a ton of bricks. Jesus Christ!

Especially after, she just finalized the changes to the prototype. Changes which will ensure it runs properly during the demo and every time after that.

It can't be.

Have I really been so blind?

Have I made the biggest mistake of my life in trusting her, bringing her into my confidence, allowing her such access to something which has meant almost as much to me as my own child? This drone and the technology behind it have the ability to make or break my company. Everything is riding on this.

And she just rode off with the man who's probably my only true enemy.

I walk back to the bank of elevators in a daze, like a man who's just been through a bombing or climbed out of car wreck. I don't know which end is up right now. I feel as if I have completely lost my grip on reality. *Sam? Sam is the leak. The rat!* I don't want to believe she could have anything to do with the leak, but it's the only answer that makes sense.

I barely feel the elevator rising up to the top floor as I go over the facts of the situation.

All right. Logic. No more thinking with my dick. Just pure logic.

No more than a few weeks after Ryland hired her—maybe a month, I'll have to check the specifics in her file—we found out about the leak when Arcane came forward with their version of my drone. Which means they had enough time to make use of the stolen plans. It isn't as though I made it easy for anyone to do it—I even made sure to order separate files for each aspect of the design: exterior, power, fuel, structure, aerodynamics. Someone would have to have accessed all of it to make use of any of it.

She could've easily done it. Ryland has access to all of the files, as does Lou, Ralph, and probably Steve. And me. We're the only five people. But she might have caught sight of Ryland while he inadvertently went through the files at some point. After all, they work very closely together and she definitely could have had access to those designs.

Now's not the time for that. I can't go to him before I have it out with her. So help me God, if she tells him what she discovered today…

By the time I reach the top floor, the numbing shock has worn off. All that is left is cold fury. That bitch. She thinks she can ruin me with her body? I never suspected her for a moment. It makes me feel sick to think of how easily she played me. Hell, I dropped into her hands like an overripe fruit.

I shake my head. Incredible. Her working for the enemy behind my back. It's almost exactly like what I did with Regina…I imagined it all in my head. She'd been so ready and willing to fuck me because she was screwing me. It would be funny if it weren't so sickening. God, she's probably sleeping with Weissman too. It turns my stomach to imagine his liver spotted hand on her creamy skin. My gut burns.

Fuck you, Sam Harper.

I slam my fist on the wall outside Erica's office. The pain radiates into my arm.

Erica comes running out, and stares at me with widened eyes. "What's the matter?" she gasps.

"Nothing," I snarl and walk past her.

I stopped thinking with my brain from the moment I saw her. Not anymore.

She has no idea who she's dealing with. Neither of them do.

SAMANTHA

The one good thing I can say about having lunch with my father is that it's at least just the two of us. No insufferable stepmother or stepsister to make things worse than they already are.

And he has to pay attention to me, for once. And why not? It'd been his idea for us to get together.

Only, I'm the one with the attention problems today. I can't stop thinking about Lincoln long enough to hold onto the thread of our conversation. I keep getting lost.

Dad doesn't look surprised. He's never been much for having faith in my intellect, after all.

Which is another reason why I wonder what this is all about. What's he getting at?

"I imagine things in the office are getting quite interesting, with the tech conference coming up like a freight train." He chuckles, as though we're sharing some great joke.

I can't help but frown. "Since when do you care what my work life is like?"

He manages to mime an expression of disappointment, his mouth curving down at the corners. "That's mean, and unfeeling. And untrue, to boot. I care very much about your work."

"That's not what you said on Friday night. In fact," I murmur, leaning closer with my arms crossed on top of the table. "You made it clear that you don't believe I could ever come up with anything worthwhile."

"I was angry. You must try to understand my position in the family. Having to sit between you and my new family. Trying to bring everyone together, trying to create a single family unit when it's so difficult to get the three of you to see eye-to-eye. I was deeply vexed, especially since you were so rude to your sister."

"Stepsister," I correct.

"Case in point," he replies, eyes narrowing. "You refuse to meet me halfway."

"So that's why you were so cruel, then? Because I made your life more difficult?"

"Of course. I would never be so unsupportive, otherwise."

What a laugh. Who does he think he's trying to fool? Like we only met yesterday. Like I haven't dealt with his complete lack of support throughout my entire life. "Very kind of you." I sit back when the server arrives with my salad, which is at least an excuse to keep from talking so much. If we're eating, there will be less of an opportunity for us to trip over our

139

words. Why wouldn't we be awkward? We barely know each other, after all.

"So, as I was saying," he continues as soon as the waiters leave, "I'm sure your work has been quite stressful lately. But stress helps move the day along, doesn't it?"

Why does he care so much? I can't make heads or tails of the way he keeps going back to work. "Yes. It's been very busy, but rewarding. I'm sure we'll come out on top." I raise an eyebrow, deciding this is the time to play my ace in the hole. To take him by surprise. "I mean, just because Arcane Technologies poached the design Lincoln created…"

I couldn't have imagined a better reaction if I tried. His eyes go wide, his pale skin goes red. Like he's ready to burst. I'm surprised steam isn't pouring from his ears. "How dare you accuse me of something like that?" he huffs.

"Because it's the truth, isn't it? I heard it through the grapevine earlier this week, after meeting with you for dinner," I challenge coolly.

He scowls angrily. "Do they know you are my daughter?"

"Don't worry, nobody knows that you're my father. If they did, I never would've gotten the job."

He visibly relaxes and even manages to force a smile. "Of course, since you took your mother's maiden name when you were sixteen."

"Of course." I silently thank my guardian angels or inner voice or whatever it was that told me to take her name. I'd much rather live the life of a normal woman than the life of Vince Weissman's daughter, no matter how many surface perks came along with that. I've always left that privilege to my many stepmothers and their children.

His color starts to return to normal. "I find it highly offensive that you would accuse me of theft."

"What is it, if not theft?" I ask. The fact is, I didn't know until just now that he'd taken Lincoln's design. It was a hunch of mine, nothing that I heard from work. I read about Arcane's test run, the same as everyone else.

"Has it ever occurred to you that my engineers were working on the same technology months before Guardian began working on it?" he asks, cutting into his steak. "Has it ever occurred to you that your boss might have stolen the idea from me?"

Unthinkable, but he doesn't know what I know about Lincoln. He's a man of character, principle. He wouldn't take the easy way out like that. If anything, he does everything the hard way. He's the most stubborn, pig-headed man I've ever known, and considering my lineage, that's saying something. "I suppose that isn't unthinkable," I lie around a mouthful of salad. Maybe he won't hear the obvious contempt in my voice if I keep my mouth full.

"I only wish we could get over the hump," he admits, shaking his head ruefully.

"The hump?"

"The temperature issues. We've been having them. I'm certain you have, too. The core temperature jumps up and fries everything." He shakes his head again.

I'm so ashamed of my father I feel as if I might throw up. My father is a thief. If he was merely researching and working on

141

technology which would make it possible for drones to travel faster and longer, why would he just so happen to come up with the same exact issue we've been battling all this time? It would mean following the exact same process of design, development, and everything else. What are the odds that his engineers designed an exact replica of the ill-informed design Lincoln created for the Excalibur GTX3?

Slim to none, that's what.

And my father is fishing for answers. I know he is. God, he has so little faith in me. It's a struggle to keep my expression neutral as I pretend to mull over his statement. "It's a challenge," I murmur with a shrug, staying as noncommittal as I can.

"I suppose that whoever comes up with a solution first will be the one to win over the investors at the demonstration," he observes, sounding as though he only just came up with this revelation on the fly. He should've taken up acting instead of stealing other people's work. He might have been more successful at it.

There are only three people who know about the exact problem we were having with the prototype: me, Lincoln and Ryland. I highly doubt that Lincoln would leak the details of his prize project to his biggest competitor, so that leaves only one person.

I feel sick at the thought. Ryland?

Is he really capable of something like this? It's hard to imagine. They are best friends and Ryland plays the nice guy so effortlessly, it is impossible to think it could be a pretense. Besides, I've come to admire him so highly since he hired me. We get along so well and he seems to have a real, deep affection for Lincoln.

Does he, though? If he did, he wouldn't have betrayed him. I know he did. It could only have been him. Maybe he's tired of playing second fiddle to his best friend. Maybe he wants a bigger piece of the action. I have to bite my tongue to keep from asking my father what he promised Ryland in exchange for his treachery.

My heart sinks even more. I realize now that he only hired me because of who I am. He must've known somehow, that I'm my father's daughter. Maybe that was why he'd been so dead set on getting me into the company. So he could use me and my connection to my father to further himself.

I slide my hands under the table, into my lap and clench them as hard as I can in an attempt to hide my rage. My palms sting when my nails sink into them, nearly drawing blood. The filthy, lying bastard. Cozying up to me in the lab, using me. Lying to Lincoln. Making him trust him, believe in him.

I'd been so wrong about him, about everything.

"What's the matter?" My father peers at me, examining me.

I'm giving myself away. "Sorry. I have a lot on my mind." Another mouthful of food. I can barely taste it anymore, and I sure as hell don't want to eat anything. I'm surprised my stomach even accepts what I swallow, I feel so sick and awful. For myself, for Lincoln, for everyone involved except for Ryland and the man seated across from me. I can't even think about him as my father anymore.

"Work, eh?" He grins, taking a huge bite of his bloody steak.

The juices drip down his chin. The sight is nauseating. He dabs it away with a snowy white napkin.

I force a faint smile and shrug. "Yes. Would I be your daughter if I didn't allow work to get in the way of a good meal?" I pretend to share a good-natured chuckle with him and lean forward with an expression of interest as he starts off on a story about his company.

I stare at him and nod at all the appropriate places. I know what this lunch is about now. It is a fishing trip for him. He wants to know what I know.

I think of Lincoln. If my father gets the design, he will be destroyed. I have to figure out a way to help him.

SAMANTHA

My stomach's in knots, tightening further every moment that passes. It's amazing I've managed to hang onto my lunch. What am I going to do?

I've paced the floor of the lab so many times, it's amazing that I haven't worn through the rubberized industrial tiles. I have to figure out a way out of this. I can't let Ryland and Dad get away with it. No way. They're the bad guys, and the bad guys shouldn't win.

I'm not a child. I know the bad guys win sometimes. Maybe even a lot of the time, since they have the resources and all that jazz. But it won't be like that this time. Not if I have anything to do with it.

I should go to Lincoln and tell him about Ryland, but accusing his best friend of corporate espionage is no joking matter. I'd better be damn sure of the truth of my accusations before I take them to him. What happens if I'm wrong? What happens if I drive a wedge between them? Neither would ever forgive me, and it would be impossible to continue working here under those conditions. I need proof of some kind.

That, combined with the fact that they might find out whose daughter I am, leaves me with very little choice. I can't go off half-cocked on this. It's too important that I get it right.

An idea starts forming in my head. Sketchy, but maybe worthwhile. Is there a way I could mix up my findings somehow? I haven't saved any of my files yet, haven't returned them to the shared folders for access by others. "Others" meaning Ryland, Lincoln, or the head of security. Even Lou doesn't know the specifics of what's wrong with the original design. I know because Ryland told me so.

I stop in the middle of the lab. How do I know I can believe anything he's ever told me?

I carry on pacing. I have to take a chance, anyway.

If Ryland doesn't know the specifics of my ultimate solution, I might be able to sabotage the information he leaks to my father. I left the real plans in Lincoln's office earlier. I could always go in and change the file, or even pretend I made a mistake...

Yes. That's the way. Can I pull it off? I need to get myself together, otherwise he'll know something's up right away. I can't let Lincoln down by screwing up something so important. I can't let Ryland know what he's done. I have to pretend nothing happened today, that I'm just as enamored of his skill and talent as I was when we last spent time together on Monday morning. We're friends, pals, conspirators working together to bring Lincoln's ultimate vision to life.

What a crock of bullshit. What would Lincoln do if he knew the truth? I don't need to think about it for too long. I stop pacing, calm myself, and to put myself in the right headspace. I have to be casual. If my father can pretend to be innocent and free of betrayal, so can I.

I go over to my computer and make two small changes to the design. One obvious and another not so obvious. Then I save the design on a USB stick and slip it into my pocket.

"Knock, knock," I murmur when I reach the open door to Ryland's office. He must have ordered lunch in. I can smell the onions on his sandwich from across the room. I wrinkle my nose, waving my hand in front of my face.

"Yeah, yeah," he laughs, shrugging. "I like 'em."

"It's a good thing you don't share this office with anyone." I chuckle. "That smell is obnoxious."

"I wouldn't get onions on it if I had to share my office," he assures me with a grin.

Aww... what a nice guy, but you'd stab your best friend in the back for money. I grin back.

"What can I do for you?"

This is it. It's now or never. "I wanted to pop my head in and confirm what I replicated this morning," I explain. "But I can come back if you're busy with your lunch."

"No, no, not at all, but that won't be necessary. Lincoln already sent me the files."

I frown. "He did."

"What's the matter?"

"Well, I made a little typo in my report," I confess, grimacing. "But I fixed it."

"A typo? That's not going to help anyone," he chides, but gently and with a smile.

And I see it then. The slimy smile. I walk over. "I know, I know. I was so excited—"

"Yes, yes, it is very exciting. What's the problem?" he asks, pushing his smelly sandwich to the side and beckoning for me to come closer.

Yeah, I'll bet he's more than happy to shove what's left of his sandwich to the side in favor of getting more information from me. *The creep. The liar. He used me.* He probably doesn't have any higher an opinion of me than my father has. Have they laughed together over how easy it is to lie to me? How easy it is to lie to Lincoln?

I hand over my USB stick.

I have to hold my breath over the scent of onions hanging heavy in the air, or maybe I just don't want to breathe in the scent of him.

He slots the USB into his computer and opens my file.

"See? I accidentally typed a one-point-two-five instead of point-one-two-five in the measurements of the new fan vent. I mean, that would be way too much. The whole thing would fall apart for lack of a properly-placed decimal point. I'd never forgive myself."

He shrugs. "No big deal. You caught it in time. Well done. I'll let the Big Boss know about it. Don't worry he won't be upset over this."

Oh, yes, you cretin. That's exactly what I'm worried about. Lincoln getting angry with me over a perceived mistake. If my calculations are correct, the openings in the vent will still be much too small to allow enough heat to exit the body of the drone. When Arcane polishes up their prototype, it'll crash during the demonstration. I hope.

It's my only hope. The only thing I can hang onto.

I flash him what I hope is a grateful smile. Exactly the sort of smile I would've given him if I didn't detest him the way I do now. "Thank you, as always. The last thing I need is for him to get on my case about yet another thing, you know?"

He sighs, folding his arms. "I've told you already. I don't want to be any part of the issues between you two. It puts me in a very uncomfortable position. I have a lot of faith in you, Sam."

Oh, sure, you do. You have faith that I'll be stupid enough to let you keep using me until my father gives you what he's promised. Whatever that happens to be. I want to ask him so badly. I want to know what could be important enough that it convinced him to betray the oldest friend he has, someone who trusts him like a brother. Judas had his thirty pieces of silver. How many pieces did Dad buy Ryland for?

"You're right, you're right," I mutter. "You know him better than I do. I bet the two of you have shared just about everything over the years. I can't come in between that."

"Nothing ever could," he replies, his face unsmiling.

"Right. Catch you later," I say walking away. I glance back at him as I reach the door.

He is watching me with a smile.

What a liar. I wonder how he can live with himself, how he can sleep at night.

Then again, I'm a liar, too. I just lied to him. I think of feeding the false information to my father as I walk back to the little office. I let the locks engage behind me before I allow myself to lean against the door, suddenly shaking from head to toe.

The tech conference is next week. One full week until the Arcane prototype fails in front of a crowd. I honestly don't know how I'll be able to wait that long, but it'll be worth it when I have real, irrefutable proof to take to Lincoln. Without that, it will be no more than my word against Ryland's, and as my boss just told me, he and Lincoln have shared everything throughout their lives.

A bitter smirk shows itself on my face when I reflect on the one thing they don't share—integrity.

LINCOLN

I feel sick to my stomach, but there's no other choice. I have to do this.

Doing it means admitting she made a fool of me, but it also means refusing to be made a fool of any longer. I have to remember this. If there's any hope of regaining my self-respect, it's in this action. About time Weissman finds out I'm onto him, that I'm not so easily fooled.

But you were easily fooled, you idiot. Look what she did to you. Look how easy it was for her to find a way into your life. Into your pants. Into your heart? That last bit is a question, taunting me. Making my skin crawl. Into my heart? Did she get there? I don't know and I'm not sure I want to ponder that just now, as I take the elevator down to the lab.

Accompanied by two security guards who will escort Miss Weissman out of my premises.

Getting rid of Regina was easy, but getting rid of Sam is another matter altogether. Her claws are deeper in my flesh. God, I hate this.

But I'm the boss, and it's my job to make the tough calls. She's lucky I believe in discretion, or I would've had her meet me in my office and paraded her through the top floor, so everyone would see, whisper and gossip behind us.

We stop outside the lab and I take a deep breath. I know she's in there. The security logs tell me she just entered not five minutes ago, and the door hasn't opened since. I use my card key to get in, swinging the door open with determination.

She lied to me.

She thought she could get away with it. Nobody gets away with trying to make a fool out of me. My hands clench into tight fists as I catch sight of her. I can see she's been deep in thought over something. The sight of her sends waves of nausea rolling through me.

Sam looks up at the sound of the door, her gaze flickering over to where the two guards are standing, one over each of my shoulders. Her frown deepens, her eyes darken. "What is this?" she whispers.

"What do you think it is?" I'm in the presence of two other employees. There can be no personal exchange here. Thank God, because seeing her again, makes me doubt my own eyes. How can she look so innocent? Yet, I saw her get into Weissman's car.

"I don't understand." She rises.

Wasn't I just inside her less than two hours ago? Wasn't it good? The best?

"It's time for you to go. Now. You're fired."

A host of emotions play upon her face, her expression

shifting back and forth. "Wh-what? Fired? What did I do?" Her eyes bore holes into me, as though asking the question she doesn't dare give voice to. Am I firing her for turning me down for lunch?

Does she think I'm that petty?

"Come on. Let's go." I'm at the end of my tether as it is, barely holding on to the last shreds of self-control. She used me. She lied. And lied. Again and again. Every damn thing was a lie. She even used my daughter to get closer to me. This realization is the final straw. I can't even look at her.

"Hurry up, please," I bark.

She fumbles for her purse, still obviously shaken by this turn of events. Did she think I would never find out? Well, I did. Weissman took a clever gamble by choosing her, but he underestimated me.

"What's going on, Lincoln?" she asks, her voice a hoarse whisper, pleading with me as she crosses the room. Not with words. With her eyes, as if she believes she deserves better than this. As though she deserves anything.

What a laugh.

"We're leaving. Now." I wave to the guards, who flank her as we exit the lab and walk down the hall. It's empty, most people probably still taking late lunches, or hard at work. Good. I don't want a scene, no matter how vile she is. I find it hard to hurt her.

"Can I at least—"

"No. You have no options here. You have no rights. You don't seem to understand how something like this works."

"How something like what works?" She turns to me as we arrive at the elevators, eyes searching my face. "What is this? What is it, really? Please."

She's a good actress. A damned good one. I can almost believe she's truly stricken with grief over this turn of events. Her eyes, when I dare to meet her gaze, are wide with emotion and sparkling with unshed tears.

Yes, she's a good actress, and she fooled you. In all probability, she's his lover. Don't forget the way his hand moved to the small of her back when he picked her up.

My heart hardens.

"I'll take it from here," I advise the guards.

They exchange a dubious look but fall back, allowing me to accompany Samantha into the elevator. Alone.

The second the doors slide shut, she whirls on me. "I know why you're doing this, but you've got it all wrong! I'm not the one who leaked the design to Weissman!"

"Ah, so you know it has to do with a leak," I snarl, eyes trained straight ahead. I won't look at her again.

"Please, please, you have to listen to me. Everything depends on this! I'm not the mole. It was Ryland all along. You have to believe me! It's Ryland, Lincoln. I didn't know it until this afternoon."

"You mean when you had lunch with Weissman?" I ask.

Sam gasps. "You know about that?"

"How else do you think I know what you've done?"

"No, no, it's not like that at all. Vince Weissman is—"

"Please, spare me the lurid details," I spit, cutting her off. "I don't need to know who you are to each other, and I don't want to know. All I know is, you took this job in order to steal the plans and give them to your boss. And then, you go ahead and blame one of my best people? My best friend, for Christ's sake? What? Did Weissman warn you that I might be getting closer to the truth? That you might have to throw somebody under the bus soon?"

"No, that's not it at all, why won't you listen to me?"

"Because you're only going to come back at me with lies, and more lies," I snarl, sounding vicious even to my own ears. But it feels good to let go of the stinging pain of betrayal. I want her to hurt, too. "You disgust me. Is there anything you'll stop at to get what you want? What your boss wants? Did he tell you to fuck me again if I got suspicious of you?"

Her head jerks back as if I'd slapped her. "How dare you?" she breathes, eyes like saucers. Hurt.

The incredible hurt I see on her face confuses me. I blink, then remember myself and force a laugh. It comes out sounding like a bark. "How dare I? That's rich, coming from a whore like you. You make me sick. Just be grateful I'm not involving the police."

She swallows, and her face pales.

Suddenly, I just want to hold her in my arms. My own weakness shames me. I lash out, "Did you use that body of yours to get in with Weissman? Is that why you're so good at it? Because you've had so much practice?"

And that was too much. I knew it when it was coming out of my mouth, and yet I let it out. I'm ashamed of myself for saying it, especially when her chin starts to quiver. My heart feels like there's a knife in it. I'm better than this—at least I thought I was. Maybe I don't know anything at all.

Sam stands her ground. "I would rather be a whore than a pig-headed idiot like you who refuses to see the truth when it's right in front of him." A solitary tear rolls down her cheek, but she doesn't brush it away. It's an accusation of my cruelty.

I shouldn't have said it. I wish I could take it back, but it's out. I frown. What the fuck am I doing feeling bad about hurting her feelings? She betrayed me. I owe her shit. If she doesn't want to be called names, she shouldn't do the things she does.

Even so…

When the elevator doors open, I realize this is it. I'll never see her again. I'll never get the chance to take back the awful things I just said. My body has a mind of its own, because before I can stop myself I'm reaching for her, wanting to apologize for my brutality.

Sam looks down at my hand and sneers, shoving it away before bolting from the elevator and running through the lobby.

I can't exactly call out to stop her, so there's no other choice but to watch her retreating figure as she runs out of my life forever.

The doors slide shut.

LINCOLN

"Hey, Daddy?"

I close my eyes momentarily. My nerves are frayed, and it's becoming increasingly difficult to hold back my irritation for all interruptions, but it's not Maddie's fault. I have to deal with this without involving her. I exhale. "Yes, honey?"

"How come I couldn't stay home with Gwen tonight?"

"She had other plans," I murmur, looking over the stack of notes I've spent the last several hours going through, to no avail, I might add. But there's got to be something here. There's just got to be. "She told us when she took the job, remember? That she had something to do tonight and couldn't spend the evening with you, but she's usually free whenever we need her."

"But she's free tomorrow?"

"Yes."

"Tomorrow is the demonstration for the prototype, right Daddy?"

"That's right." Every time I think about tomorrow, my chest tightens. The thought of my little girl being without a parent is the only thing keeping me from letting the stress take over completely. I'll end up giving myself a stroke if I'm not careful. Where would that leave her?

She's sitting on a chair by the window, looking out, kicking her feet back and forth. Patient, for the most part.

I remind myself that she's much more patient than I would have been in her situation. At her age, I was fucking bouncing off the walls. "I'm sorry to make you hang around the office with me," I say, chastised in the face of her sweet complacency.

"It's okay." She smiles at her reflection in the window.

"It's just tonight. Tomorrow, you'll be with Gwen for most of the day, and then..." And then, I don't know what will happen. If we go bust, I'll have a lot more time to spend with her. Maybe that's not a bad thing. Not for her, anyway. Not in the immediate future. Long term, well, that's another story. "We'll be doing lots of things together."

"Until it's time for me to go back to school again and make new friends," she says, in a happy voice.

"That's right, honey." I look away from her back and carry on pouring over Sam's notes like the rest of like my life depends on it. Because it does. Mine, the company's, my daughter's. At the back of my mind is the fear that I never knew Sam, so I can't trust my own judgement of her. What if she sabotaged the work in some small way? That is what I would have done if I were in her shoes.

"Is Sam working downstairs?"

An inexplicable hollow sense of sadness and loss fills my heart. I take a deep breath. If only my daughter knew what she's doing to me by asking such innocent questions. "No, baby. She's not."

"How do you know?"

"I just do."

"Can we go and look?" she insists.

My head whirls around in the direction of my daughter. "Maddie, enough."

I hate the look of surprise and guilt in her eyes when I glare at her, and instantly my anger dissipates. "I'm sorry. I don't mean to be short with you. But you know how busy I am tonight. You'll just have to take my word for it. Sam is not working downstairs." Anymore. Not that her physical absence has done anything to remove her from my mind. She might as well be standing in front of me, right here and now. That's how strongly I feel her presence.

She blinks hard. "Sorry, Daddy. I just wanted to say hello."

"I'm sure she would like to see you too," I say, swallowing back my disgust at myself. Why did I let my daughter meet her? No woman will ever get that opportunity again, until she has proven her worth. When I think of how Sam cozied up to my daughter, all in effort to get closer to me, it makes me rage all over again.

Then, I remember how gentle she was when she washed

Maddie's face and feet after we got back from the fair. How she held her hand throughout the day, how the two of them giggled over the clowns and the street artists. There was a naturalness to their interactions. Nothing forced, nothing over-the-top. Nothing done for my benefit.

All right, so she's not a complete monster. The kid is charming and sweet, anybody with even a portion of a heart would fall for a kid like her. And that's true. I believe it. Sam didn't use Maddie to get to me.

Even so, that doesn't erase the fact that she's a thief. I lost millions because she stole our design and gave it to Weiss-man. And the fact that she is downright dangerous. She tried to blame the leak on Ryland. As if Ryland would ever do something like that to me. I'm sure she saw the opportunity to create even more chaos by splitting us up and pounced on it. It's a Weissman move all the way.

Ryland seemed to be even more enraged than I was when I came clean about her. He stood so abruptly, his chair slammed against the wall behind him. "That bitch!" he'd shouted, face red as a lobster. "Who the hell does she think she is? And that bastard, Weissman. I could kill him for this."

I almost forgot my own pain watching him go off like that. He then went on to trash talk Sam for at least another thirty minutes, ranting and raving about how she wasn't even that strong as an engineer. That bothered me then and it bothers me now, though I kept my mouth shut. I've always been the type to go overboard, to get a little too intense, but him? He's always so laid back he's in danger of bedsores. All the time I've known him, he's always been the one to pull me back, level me out, and when necessary, remind me I was acting like a jackass.

So what's with the sudden change of heart? Why so vicious about Sam?

He can't possible feel as betrayed as I do. Maybe because he put his ass on the line for her, fought for me to hire her, to keep her on even when she pissed me off. He's done nothing but praise her since the moment she walked through the doors. Why else would he turn on her so quickly? That's got to be it.

Unless…

I shake my head, running my hands through my hair and scrubbing them over my scalp in a confused daze.

No. There's no way.

He's my buddy.

I've known him since school days. He wouldn't betray me like that. Why would he? What reason could there be? We've never been anything but best friends from the day we met. There's never even been a hint of rivalry between us. I've treated him practically as a partner in the company, with a salary to match. When we were first starting up and money was tight, I took the pay cut and let him take home the bigger salary. His eleven percent of company shares mean he stands to make millions from this technology. There is no reason on earth for him to want this company to fail. It's his hard work too.

Even so…

Something niggles at the back of my brain. Why didn't he at least try to defend her even a little? It's not as though I had literal proof that she was the one and only mole in the company. He never once tried to get me to stand back and take another look, when he almost never misses an opportunity to suggest just that. No, instead, he derided her work. He all but erased the progress she made. And it was her progress, entirely. Her notes tell me so. She's not a stupid girl, she's not a poor engineer, but he was suspiciously quick to categorize her as such.

Why?

I drop my head in my hands. *Fuck, fuck, fuck*. She's still in my head. Making me doubt Ryland, screwing with my sense of loyalty and justice.

"Daddy?"

I lift my head and look at Maddie. "Hmm?"

"Are you all right?" she asks worriedly.

"Yes, I'm just tired.

"I'm pretty tired. Can we go home now?"

At least, she trusts me enough now to admit when she's tired, instead of crawling into a corner and falling asleep on her own. She knows it's no crime to be sleepy, that I won't be angry with her.

I nod, suddenly very tired myself. "Okay, honey. We'll get going in just a minute. Let me check my email once more, and we'll head out."

She nods, and I turn my attention back to the computer.

One particular name in the list of senders stands out, and I have to grit my teeth against the gasp of surprise. She has balls...I'll give her that. I'm surprised she contacted me tonight, but I can't pretend I'm not eager to see what she has to say. I open Sam's email and begin to read.

I'm sure you don't want to hear from me—tonight of all nights. You must be working hard to get everything in place for tomorrow. I thought I would be there with you. It was my baby too.

But it's okay. I understand your reaction, now that I've had time to think it over.

First and foremost, I should've been honest with you from the beginning. I should've told you Vince Weissman is my father.

"What?" I blurt out, reading the line again, my jaw hanging open.

"Huh?" Maddie asks.

"Nothing, darling."

My father and I have never had a relationship, and he's certainly never showed an interest in my work. I never thought he would have any sort of effect on my life, so I figured it wasn't worth mentioning. Besides, would you have hired me if you knew who he was? I doubt it. I took my mother's maiden name when I turned sixteen, determined to strike out on my own without the family name hanging over my head. I didn't want any preferential treatment. You understand. Of all people, I feel like you would.

And I do. If what she's saying is true, I now understand why she seemed to relate to my daughter's pitiful childhood up to this point. I can't imagine having a father like him, the slime.

When he asked me to lunch that day, I was sure there had to be some ulterior motive behind it. We're not the daddy buying lunch for his darling daughter types. Sure enough, when he kept peppering me with questions about Excalibur—specifically how it was coming along, whether we were ready for the demo—I knew something was up. I'd heard rumors of him stealing the plans for the other drone, and I carried those rumors in my heart up until that lunch date. When I confronted him, he claimed you were the one who stole the plans from him.

"That bastard," I mutter, then glance at my daughter.

She shakes her head, waving a finger back and forth in admonishment. "That's a bad word, Daddy."

"Sorry," I whisper and go back to the email.

I know his version of the story can't possibly be true, or else how is it possible that both companies are having the same problems with cooling? It was a bit too much of a coincidence for me. His engineers, if they really were working on the technology for months prior to your development of the drone, would have worked out such bugs before now. But I knew they hadn't, because he kept alluding to the problem, and trying in a roundabout way to see whether I'd come up with a solution.

I knew then that only two people could've leaked the plans to him. It couldn't be you, since that would mean sabotaging your own company. It had to be Ryland. He's the only one working as close to the project as I am, and he would have easy access to all my files.

You don't want to believe me. I get that. I do. I didn't want to believe it at first, either. After all, he's been my mentor. He insisted I work for your company. I know now that his advocacy was calculated. Not so great for my ego, to put it mildly, but I'll get over it.

There's one way for you to be sure that I'm telling the truth, however, and it also happens to be the way we can put an end to this madness. I only hope it works out the way I planned it.

I gave Ryland the wrong information on the changes we made to the body of the drone, specifically, the alterations to the fan vent. If he did indeed, give that information to my father, their version of the drone should still overheat.

Rest assured, the correct calculations are still in the files containing my notes and the plans. I can't imagine Ryland changing them to reflect what I told him, since that would mean having the correct information on record. He would want the wrong measurements to be used, so your drone would crash and Arcane's would fly.

I have to think this through. Is she truly onto something? What she's saying makes sense, in that Ryland would want Arcane to have the correct numbers while leaving us with something which could sink the entire project.

Adrenaline races through my veins. I want her to be right. God, how I want her to be right, but being right would mean that Ryland is a traitor. All these years, I kept a viper close to my heart. If she is right, it means we would win out over Arcane. And it would mean that Sam was telling the truth all along.

I'm sorry for the way this worked out, Lincoln. I wish you nothing but luck tomorrow. Goodbye.

I close the email and flop backwards into my chair. Hope bubbles up like an underground spring. If she's telling the truth and there is no reason for her to write this email tonight, then there's still a chance for success. For tomorrow to be a success, tonight is crucial. I need evidence and I'm going to find it.

I shoot Maddie an apologetic look. "Sorry, kiddo. It's going to be a slightly longer night than I'd anticipated. Tell you what, I'll dig your Princess bed out and build it up for you.

Then we can curl up together, and I'll read you a bedtime story before you go to sleep?"

"My Princess bed?"

I grin at her. "Yup."

"Yay, Daddy."

LINCOLN

If there wasn't so much nervous energy pumping through my veins, combined with caffeine, I might be dragging my feet. At seven this morning, I carried my sleeping daughter into her bed. I then waited for her nanny to come through the door before going back to the office.

I know I look like death warmed over, a sleepless night is hardly the ideal situation before a day as important as this one, but if I pull this off, then I'm set for life.

I have to crush this.

It will go well. It has to.

So why is my stomach in such a tight knot?

I watch people filing into the room. They're from all walks of life, really—investors, enthusiasts, tech writers. The conference draws thousands of people from around the world every year. There's always plenty of excitement when it comes to getting the first look at a new piece of technology.

It's a theater in the round, with multiple levels of seating arranged in a circle around the room. As the minutes tick by, the buzz grows.

I'm still not completely sure Sam is telling the truth and won't be until Weissman's people demonstrate, but a little faith never hurt anybody. Especially after what I found out last night. Access logs and security tapes having been flawlessly doctored. Lou would never have noticed, and I might have missed it too, but I know my lab inside out. I know the vents open at only certain times and they seemed to be opening at the wrong times.

Some of these doctored tapes dated before Sam even started working for me.

I still don't know why Ryland would do it, though. This is what sticks in my craw as I stand behind the curtain separating those of us preparing for demonstrations from the hundreds of spectators filling the seats. Why would he go behind my back this way? What did I ever do to him? And he sat there, just as surprised and offended as anybody, when we found out Weissman had stolen our design.

No. My design.

Ryland, my best friend. My buddy. It has to be him. Only he knew enough about the design to take it to someone else. He maneuvered Sam's hiring in the company. She was the perfect decoy, wasn't she? They could blame it all on her.

Which reminds me.

I peer through the opening in the curtains, scanning the room for any sign of Weissman. He'll be out there, naturally, since his corporation is performing a demo. He'll want to witness his triumph over his biggest competitor in person.

Not just the success of his drone, but the destruction of mine.

He might be in for quite a surprise.

Ryland approaches, grinning from ear to ear.

I stare at him. Still not wanting to believe how wrong I've been. His smile is so real, so full of pride I could actually believe he's my friend. I've seen that grin so many times. Before a game, before an important presentation, when he stood as my best man. If it weren't for Sam, I wouldn't have the slightest clue of what might be behind that grin. Those friendly eyes.

"Ready for this?" he asks, his voice full of excitement.

Is it excitement at the thought of seeing me fail? It has to be. Does he secretly hate me that much? It might not even be personal, really. Maybe he's just collecting a hefty payday from Weissman, of a bigger share of Weissman's company, once mine has been destroyed. Who knows? I want so much to ask him about the tapes. I want to ask what I did to leave him so vulnerable to bribery, if that's what this is all about, but I don't. I turn away from him. I actually can't look at him.

"As ready as I'll ever be," I murmur, looking out over the audience again.

"You're nervous?"

"Yeah." I don't turn to face him. He might be able to read me if I look him in the eye. Let him think I'm having a bad case of nerves and leave it at that.

"Don't worry. Your drone will kill it." He slaps my back.

My first instinct is to turn around and sock him in the jaw.

But I don't. Soon, he will be nothing to me. What is important is my company. My eyes catch movement.

There he is. The smug son of a bitch, moving toward his seat in the front row. Very good, Vince, very good. All the better to watch me destroy you.

I wish Sam were here. Damn it, why was I so quick to judge her? I pushed her away out of hurt and rage. Even though I called her a whore—something I still haven't forgiven myself for—she reached out to me and clued me in on the trick she played on Ryland. She didn't have to do that. She could've left me to my own devices. She could've hung me out to dry.

"Looks like we're up before Arcane," Ryland whispers, standing close to me.

I force myself not to move away. I turn to look at him, my face composed. He is going to get such a shock. "Good, because I don't feel like waiting for them to get through their presentation before I get through ours." And it'll look better for me to present first, too. They'll be the ones who look like thieves—which is what they are.

"Wait. What?" It's a sharp question, surprised. Dismayed, even.

"Yeah, I'm running the demonstration, myself."

He frowns suspiciously. "But I've been rehearsing it for days."

"I'm sure you have, but nobody knows more about *my* drone than I do. It's my baby and has been from the beginning. I'm presenting." I glance at him from the corner of my eye, almost daring him to defy me on this. I wouldn't want to tip my hand too early, but he's pushing me to the breaking point.

He sees this, too, knows me well enough to know when I've had just about enough. He nods. "All right. Go for it. Good luck."

I wish I believed he really wants me to do well. It's a soul-destroying feeling when the person you loved like brother for as far back as you can remember—turns out to be your enemy.

The host of the presentation is stepping out onto the stage now, to the applause of the audience. They're ready to be wowed—well, I have a feeling they'll get what they came for.

"First up today is Guardian Technologies, presenting their design for a long-range drone."

More applause.

The knot in my stomach is as tight as it's ever been. Maybe tighter.

I carry the drone out to the stage, smiling. Nobody has touched it today except for me. I won't take any chances. This is it. Everything we've worked toward, everything we've dreamed of. The entire future of my company and everyone who works in it.

Yeah. No pressure.

I place the drone on the table and get an image of Sam in my head. She should be here with me. If this presentation goes successfully, it's because of her. Not me. She saved us. I owe her big time.

I scan the room, searching the crowd. They're an eager, captive audience. And the most eager member isn't Weiss-man, either.

It's his daughter.

There she is, up top, standing with her back to the wall. Directly across from where I'm standing now. Arms folded, eyes boring holes into me. When I look into them, she lifts her chin in that defiant way of hers. Daring me to make a scene, to call her out. To even give an indication that I know her.

I wish I could tell her I believe her, but not until I see what Arcane does. But I believe her when she says she didn't want to hurt me. I believe she didn't use me the way I accused her of doing.

There's only one way to find out if she's telling the truth about the rest of it.

My smile widens. "Good afternoon, ladies and gentlemen."

LINCOLN

"So, thanks to this breakthrough technology, our Excalibur GTX3 will be able to travel up to twenty times further than current models of even the highest-priced devices." I use the controls to raise the height at which the prototype hovers over the room. "It is also able to maintain altitude with up to ten pounds attached, without affecting the distance it can travel."

I scan the front row, pointedly meeting Weissman's gaze before looking to the person seated beside him. "Would you do me the honor of assisting me in this demonstration?"

The woman smiles, smoothing down her pencil skirt before standing. I wave her over to me, still with the controls in my hand, and point to the gallon of milk on the floor. I've been flying the drone for over ten minutes now with fifteen minutes being the longest a presentation can run. The proto-type seems to be doing just fine. *You did it, Sam. You did it.* I don't dare raise my eyes up in her direction, but I hope she feels the pride I do.

"Could you please confirm that this carton is full and not empty?" I ask, flashing her my most winning smile.

She bends, lifting the carton, and nods. "It's full of milk," she confirms with a laugh.

A general rumble of laughter spreads over the room.

"Now, would you be so kind as to hook it onto the bottom of the Excalibur GTX3?" While she's doing this, I turn to the audience. "A gallon weighs approximately eight-point-three-five pounds. Short of our ten-pound limit, but you get the idea."

More good-natured laughter.

Now, for the real challenge. I thank the volunteer and raise the drone again, this time flying it out over the crowd.

They react with squeals, shouts and laughter as they cover their heads, hoping not to get caught in a milk shower should the drone fail.

It doesn't fail.

My fifteen minutes are nearly up, and it's with a sense of joy and pride that I conclude it with, "The Excalibur GTX3 will revolutionize the way online retailers deliver products to the homes of their faithful customers. Same-day delivery no longer has to be nothing more than a pipe dream for many. It can now be a reality for a greater number of retailers and customers than ever before. Thank you so much for attending Guardian Technologies' presentation. I'll be available for questions after the other presentations are complete."

The crowd responds with resounding applause which rings

in my ears long after I've brought the drone backstage with me. Only now, can I breathe a sigh of relief, my legs are suddenly as weak as they were when I ran a marathon. I might as well have run it, come to think of it. This entire process has been just about as grueling.

Where's Ryland? I look around, finally finding him lurking deep in the shadows. I don't think I've ever seen anyone look as distressed as he does. What did he expect? He has to know that Sam's work was successful. The work which did not carry the alteration.

A smile quickly takes the place of distress. "You did it, buddy," he rejoices, clapping a hand over my shoulder. "You did it."

"We did it," I correct him. Though, I don't mean him. I mean Sam and me. The drone would've crashed and burned if it hadn't been for her tireless efforts. "But we're not out of the woods yet. We still have to see how Arcane does."

"We came first," he reminds me.

And he's right, for once. We went first. They'll remember us, no matter how Arcane's demonstration goes.

And it's up next.

After a few minutes go by, I don't even know where Ryland is as Weissman's employee gets started. He's probably lurking somewhere, watching from another angle, unwilling or unable to be too close to me when it's all on the line like this. A shame, because I would like to watch his reaction should the drone fail.

I look out over the crowd and it's obvious they're scratching their heads, wondering why they feel like they've seen this before. Not that Weissman was stupid enough to lift the verbiage of our presentation or anything, but the technology is literally the same. "That's right," I whisper, watching with a smirk. "You've seen this before. They're thieves. Unoriginal hacks."

The digital clock mounted to the floor at the edge of the stage reads eight minutes. The drone is still in-flight. Doubt wraps itself around my heart. Is it going to succeed, after all? Did Ryland clue into the way Sam lied to him? Did she lie, or was that all a story to throw me off-track?

Have I been unfairly accusing my best friend ever since last night?

Nine minutes. Ten. Fifteen. Jesus Christ. Sam lied.

I look towards the back where she was standing and she's no longer there. I stare at Weissman's drone in a daze. I was so sure of Sam. My heart feels as if it is being chewed up.

Suddenly, a voice fills the auditorium. A voice I've dreamed about. I twist my head in the direction of it.

Sam is standing at the edge of the stage holding a mike. "That's all great," she says. "Now, let's see how this drone does when it is not flying, but has to hover for more than ten minutes."

Weissman's team starts looking at each other in consternation.

The crowd starts murmuring.

"Go on, show us how your drone will perform if it is forced to hover and not fly."

Someone in the audience speaks up, "Yes, let's see that function work."

Weissman's team has no choice but to comply. They let their drone hover.

At nine-and-fifteen, I hear it. A spark. And I'm not the only one, as several of the people close to where the drone currently hovers start looking nervous. A few cover their heads with their arms. Nobody is laughing, as they were when I dangled a gallon of milk over their heads.

A spark becomes a small flame, which becomes a bigger flame. Panic begins to spread as people jump from their seats, climbing over each other and running for the doors as the drone plummets in a cloud of smoke and fire. Panicked screams fill the room faster than the smoke.

"What is this?" Weissman bellows, jumping up in outrage.

I know what it is. It's just desserts.

LINCOLN

Where the hell did she go? It never even crosses my mind that she could be one of the spectators who ran from the room in a panic when the drone burst into flames? She's seen enough drones crash and burn to fear that. Besides, she would've wanted to stay and watch the chaos and her father's absolutely epic meltdown.

I look around the lobby, the crowd looks as if they're still in shock after what just happened. An employee of the convention center ran in and used the extinguisher on the drone, which was nothing but a melted lump of plastic and metal by the time the fire went out.

I couldn't have planned it better myself, honestly. Even in my wildest dreams, they wouldn't have crashed and burned so spectacularly.

No pun intended.

"What about his drone? Can his drone pass the hover test?" Weissman screams.

My drone passes the hover test easily and I can't help but grin as I continue to scan the lobby for any sign of Samantha. I need to apologize for being the biggest blockhead the world has ever known. I would give her just about anything right now, but it wouldn't be enough.

It's not Sam that my gaze finds. It's Ryland.

Followed by Weissman.

They don't think anybody's watching as they duck through a door labeled "Employees Only."

But I am. I follow them, darting through the crowd, and hurry quickly down a corridor. They don't go too far, only towards the boiler room of the building. I press myself to the wall, watching them through the machinery.

"What the hell was that all about?" Weissman roars, hands rising up as if he wants to strike Ryland. "Do you know what a fool you just made of me in there? You're the one who gave me the plans. You're the one who assured me this would go off without a hitch. Were you trying to make a fool of me all along?"

"I'm sorry. I don't understand what happened any more than you do!" Ryland says, sounding more dismayed than I've ever heard him in all our years of supposed friendship. "Samantha was the one who provided the data, she's the one who gave me the dimensions for the tweak in the body of the drone. I only gave you what she gave me! It should've worked, damn it! I was with her before the holiday, we tested it ourselves. It worked in the lab! It worked for him!"

I know that he means me.

"Then she lied to you, didn't she?" Weissman snarls. "Or she's

just smarter than you, and she screwed something up delib-
erately. I told you it wouldn't work, bringing her in. You
should've done this on your own, the way I wanted you to
from the beginning."

Which makes it sound as though Ryland was a partner in all
of this, instead of an accomplice. God damn him. Even up
until now, part of me didn't want to believe he was capable of
such a thing. I wanted to believe that he'd been tricked, that
he had no choice, that there were extenuating circumstances
which would mean he wasn't exactly guilty. Will I ever learn
to stop seeing only what I want to see?

"All that money! All that work! All of it, down the drain,
Along with my reputation, all the contracts we were going to
land because of this! Millions of dollars. We'll never get a
single investor to back us once word gets out of what just
happened in there, you witless wonder. You failed. You're
nothing but a stupid, ungrateful, failure!"

I leave the room with Weissman's words ringing in my ears. I
don't want to hear anymore, nor do I need to. He's told me
everything I needed to hear.

"Mr. Cage! Mr. Cage!"

I barely have time to take another breath upon stepping back
into the lobby before I'm bombarded by excited attendees.

But none of them are Sam, and she's the only person I want
to see.

SAMANTHA

GUARDIAN SUES ARCANE FOR PATENT INFRINGEMENT

The headline makes my head buzz with excitement. He's really doing it, just like I'd hoped he would. He's suing my lying, cheating jerk of a father for all he's worth, which admittedly, isn't much after his epic failure at the conference.

If words were weapons, he would've beaten me beyond recognition when I confronted him the day after the ill-fated demonstration. As it is, my pride still stings a little, even though I've stopped caring about his opinion of me. But nobody, no matter how hard-hearted, can escape a verbal beating like that without a psyche wound or two.

"You." The word was a curse, delivered with all of my father's not-inconsiderable ire, when I stepped into his office. Disgust was written all over his face, the corner of his upper lip lifted in a snarl.

"Me," I replied with a slight shrug.

"How could a little nobody like you manage to double-cross me like that? You chose that bastard over me, your own father, didn't you?"

I swallowed my rising rage. How could my own father speak to me that way? How could he hate me so much? What did I ever do to make him care so little about me, my life, my feelings? "Why do you hate me so much, Dad? What have I ever done to you?"

"You want to know the truth. I hate you because you look like her."

I stare at him in astonishment. All these years and he has never once spoken to me about my mother. "What did she do to you?"

"She left me." His tone is cold and hard. "The airhead didn't know which side of her bread was buttered. And you are exactly the same."

"Maybe I'm not as stupid as you thought," I whispered, willing my voice not to shake. "Or, perhaps you're even more witless than I am. I mean, it wasn't difficult for me to get the upper hand once I knew the score."

"And you would ruin me that way? Your own flesh and blood? You would allow my business to crumble, all because you felt the need to prove something?"

I shook my head slowly, even sorrowfully. He would never get it. Everything was about him, always. The ultimate narcissist. "What makes you think I wanted to prove anything to you? What makes you think anything I do has anything to do with you anymore? I wanted to do the right

SINGLE DAD

thing, to see the right person win out. Lincoln deserved to win. It was his idea, something he worked hard on. I would've done anything to make sure the bad guy didn't profit from something he had no hand in."

He stared at me for a long, silent moment before clapping. Slowly. Sarcastically. "My, my. You're quite the heroine, aren't you?"

"The heroine who knew how to fool you, anyway," I replied. "I guess that's as heroic as I needed to be."

"We'll see how heroic you are when you see my Will."

I laughed. "You think I care about that? You never knew me at all. Not like you ever made an attempt to get to know me. I don't need your money, and I don't want it."

"Right," he sneered.

"I mean it. I'm doing just fine on my own. Now that the world knows about the Excalibur GTX3 and my role in its creation, because Lincoln has been generous enough to drop my name, but you probably know that by now. I've had more requests to consult on more design projects than I know what to do with."

"I won't wish you well," he said and turned away from me.

This was the end. If anything, he made it easy for me to walk away from him, from any chance of having a relationship with him. There's nothing between us. "I have a feeling I'll have better luck than you will." I smiled to this rigid back before turning away, and closing the door between us forever.

Now, I sit here and read the headline again, then skim the

contents of the article as I sit at my usual table. I hope Lincoln cleans Arcane out and grinds it into the dust. We haven't smoothed things over between us, and I don't know if we ever can, after all the horrible things that have gone on between us, but he did make it a point to spread the word that I played a major role in the prototype's success. He didn't have to do that. Just another example of how vastly different he is from my father, who would've taken all the glory for himself without a second thought.

The case will never make it to court, of course. The article hints at the strong possibility that it'll be settled privately. A shame, actually, since my father deserves to be on the witness stand having to sweat bullets.

Ryland, on the other hand, will go on trial, having been arrested for corporate espionage. I can't believe I ever looked up to him. My heart aches for Lincoln, who cared about him much more than I ever did.

My heart aches for Lincoln, period.

SAMANTHA

I t's a hot day, well into the nineties before noon. "Thank God for air conditioning," I whisper, cranking it up a bit more to keep the apartment comfortable on cleaning day. One of the perks of working for myself now, is having time to keep my place clean. One of the downfalls is having no excuse on the weekend to avoid cleaning my place. My cleaning sessions are almost as good as an actual workout.

When the doorbell rings, I'm on my knees on the kitchen floor with a scrub brush in one hand. "Who the heck is this?" I mutter, dropping the brush into the bucket of sudsy water and wiping the sweat from my forehead with the back of my forearm as I walk to the door. I'm not expecting anything, or anyone.

And I sure as hell am not expecting Lincoln and Maddie. Not in a million years.

"What are you guys doing here?" I ask, suddenly intensely conscious of my ratty sweats and bleach-stained tank top. My hair's in a messy bun on top of my head, strands falling out all over the place. Probably stuck to the back of my neck with sweat too.

Maddie giggles, holding her father's hand. "We came to see you!"

"I can see that," I say, smiling, looking from her to Lincoln. I don't feel like smiling at him right now. He could've called. He could've given me a little warning. And he could've refrained from bringing his daughter with him, like I'm going to soften just because she's here. He should know me better than that.

"Can we come in?" he asks, eyebrows raised.

"It doesn't look as though I have much of a choice," I murmur, stepping aside to let them in.

"Oh Sam, your apartment is so cute!" Maddie gushes, her eyes big and excited.

I'm glad I'm almost finished with the cleaning. I don't have to be embarrassed by dust bunnies under the sofa. "You like it, huh?" I chuckle, hands on my hips. "It's nearly as big as your Princess tent."

"No, it's not," she says seriously. "My tent is muuuuch smaller."

I absolutely adore this kid. She's so cute. "Make yourself comfortable," I encourage her, still side-eyeing Lincoln at the same time. I don't know what game he thinks he's playing, even though the sight of him—the fact that he's here in my apartment—makes my heart race.

I can't pretend I didn't develop feelings for him.

"I don't think I should," she says, smiling ever so slightly.

"Why not?"

Another knock at the door. I turn to it, surprised, and hear Maddie explain, "I have another appointment to go to. I'm pretty busy."

I have to laugh as I open the door to find a kindly middle-aged woman standing in the hall.

"I'm here to pick up Maddie," she explains.

Maddie runs to the door and flings her arms around the lady's waist.

"This is Gwen, Maddie's nanny." Lincoln pats the top of Maddie's head.

"I see." And I can see that he brought his daughter as a way to get in the door. Now that he's in, he can send her off with Gwen. My heart is thumping with a strange excitement, but I'm not sure how I feel about this bit of trickery. Does he think he can just roll in here and take up where we left off?

"Sam, will you come over to our house soon? Please?" Maddie asks.

"I'll see what I can do," I reply, stroking her hair before Gwen leads her away.

Leaving only Lincoln and me.

I wait until the door is closed before I whirl on him. "What do you think you're doing here?" I ask, my voice shrill with nervousness. "How manipulative can you possibly be?"

"What? You think I'm trying to manipulate you?"

I fold my arms across my chest and raise my eyebrows disbelievingly. He knew exactly what he was doing. "By bringing the baby."

"She's been driving me insane for two weeks, asking every day when we'll be able to see you again. If I didn't bring her with me, even so she could see you for a few minutes, I'd never hear the end of it. If anything, I'm the victim here," he says with a hangdog expression.

The idea of him being a victim is so ridiculous, I burst out laughing. "You're crazy."

"Yeah, I know. Crazy for you."

I pretend not to hear the last part even though my heart is singing. "Even so, I don't have to listen to a word you say. You know that, right? I could throw you out right now and have every right to do so. Nobody would blame me."

"I won't leave until you hear me out. Please, Samantha? I want to apologize."

"You could have done that over the phone." But my resolve is weakening every moment, every time our eyes meet. It's not fair. He's too sexy, too handsome, too magnetic, too everything. How am I supposed to fight that kind of pressure?

"Yeah, I could have, but I'm here now, aren't I?"

It's exhausting, trying to win. I should just give up. "Okay. You're here now. What do you have to say?" I'm careful to keep my arms folded tight in front of me, unwilling to leave myself open to him. He needs to know how much he hurt me. I can't make it easy.

To my surprise, he stumbles over his words. "I don't—I don't know where to s-start."

"You could start by telling me how wrong it was to call me what you did. That's a good start."

A dull red flush stains his cheekbones. "I should never have called you that. I'm really sorry. It's unforgivable, I know. And I know now that you were right all along. I heard your father fighting with Ryland after their demo, and it was all just like you said."

"So…?"

"So?"

I shrug. "What's all this mean? You were wrong. I knew you were wrong from the beginning, but that doesn't change the way you treated me, the things you said. How small you made me feel that day, after—after everything." My cheeks start burning at the mere mention of what went on in his office only hours before he fired me.

"I realize that," he mutters, shaking his head. "It was wrong. I can't tell you how wrong I was or how sorry I am. I was deeply hurt by what I thought was your betrayal, Sam. It cut me to the bone to think that you were not what I thought you were. Not to mention the fact that so much of the business relied on our demonstration. What would you do in my shoes?"

"I would ask why you were with Vince Weissman. I would ask flat-out if you had anything to do with the leak."

"Why would you have admitted having anything to do with it if you were really a spy? Why would you tell the truth?"

"If you had an explanation for what was happening the way I did with Ryland you would've at least gotten the chance to share it. You could've had your say. I didn't get to have mine.

I had to email you, hoping you would read it without deleting it first."

"I did." He looks and sounds sincere. I have to give him that. "I would do anything to make this up to you. Do you know that?" He takes one step closer, then another. "I mean it. Anything in the world."

I could move away, but I don't. Having him nearer to me is a joy I don't really want to refuse. I've been refusing myself for too long already. The weeks without him have been worse than torture. Even though I haven't known him for much longer than that, the heart wants what it wants.

So does the body.

"Sam. I couldn't have done anything I did without you."

When he reaches for me, I don't pull away. I allow his hands to linger on my arms—light, gentle, not demanding a thing.

"You're the entire reason we were a success at the confer- ence. It was all you. I would be nowhere without you. I'm nowhere without you now."

"What are you saying?" I whisper, not daring to hope.

"First of all, I would love it if you would come to work for me again, because you're really and truly a genius, and I need you on my team." He strokes my arms, staring deep into my eyes.

I can hardly hear him over the sound of blood rushing in my ears. Does he have any idea what he does to me? He can't possibly. I narrow my eyes until they're practically slits, pretending to think it over. He deserves to sweat a little after what he put me through. "Hmm…no. I don't think so."

"What?" He frowns and pulls back a little, hurt and surprise in his eyes.

He thought I would give in so easily, did he? "Well, I mean, I'd be happy to work *with* you. Just not *for* you. I have my own clients now."

"You do?" He looks deflated, but when he sees me raise my eyebrows, his expression changes to excitement. "That's terrific news!"

"Yes, it is. You helped quite a lot, dropping my name the way you did. I appreciate it more than I can say." I take a deep breath, releasing it slowly before continuing, "I've been wanting to get out of my father's shadow for as long as I can remember. I've wanted to make a life for myself away from him, completely and totally. And there's no way he'd ever let me into his life after what he knows I did to him, so…"

"Actually, even though I'm crushed at the thought that you won't be in the lab at all hours of the night, I'm very proud of you," he whispers, smiling softly, his eyes shining.

I'm not used to hearing people say they're proud of me. It sounds good. I could get used to it. "There's another thing, too," I whisper back, leaning in ever so slightly.

"What's that?" he asks with a totally sexy grin.

"I don't think it would be a good idea for me to date my boss."

His grin turns to a smile, wider than any I've ever seen from him. "You mean that?"

"I absolutely do."

He takes my face in his hands, cupping it gently. "In that case,

Miss Harper, I'm afraid your services will no longer be required by Guardian."

"Gee, that's a shame, but thank you for letting me know, Mr. Cage."

"Now, that we have established you are no longer working for me, Ms. Harper. I'm afraid I'm going to need to get my tongue into your sweet pussy."

I giggle, letting him pull me closer. "I'm pretty gross right now, by the way."

"There are two ways around that problem. I could lick you clean or I can get you showered up, then," he murmurs, sliding his hands over my back.

"You would lick me even though I smell of sweat and bleach?"

"Sweetness, I would take you any old way I can. I love you clean, I love you dirty, I love you drenched in sweat and stained with bleach. Anyway, I can take you."

I can hardly believe my ears. "What? You love me?"

He smiles, the slowest, sexiest smile you ever saw and I wait with bated breath for it to finish.

"I do. I really do."

"When did you realize that?"

"I think it was when you were cleaning Maddie's feet. I looked down at both your heads so close together and this strange thought crossed my mind. If any man ever hurts either of these two girls I'll fucking kill him. I felt so protective towards both of you. As if you were both mine. But of course, you were always running hot and cold, so I talked myself out of it. I told myself it was just a thing. A fling."

"I was running hot and cold because I was scared. I didn't know if—"

"I would respect you in the morning," he interrupts in a dry voice.

I smack his chest. "See these are the kinds of things that made me run hot and cold."

"I could be that guy who professes to love a woman and never hears it back, but you know, it would be nice if the feeling was returned in some small measure." He is joking, but his eyes are serious and almost apprehensive.

My chest feels like it's about to burst. Everything I've ever wanted is right here in this room, holding me in his arms. Just when I thought I lost out on my dreams of him, he came back.

"I love you, too," I breathe the words out, my eyes filling with tears in the instant before his mouth touches mine.

LINCOLN

A MONTH LATER...

"Come here," I growl at her as soon as the door is shut. She looks so fucking good in that dress.

Sam doesn't hesitate, pressing her body hard against mine, so I can feel every contour of her.

I love the way she feels. "Fuck, I want to tear this thing off of you," I mutter into her ear as I draw her close to me, brushing my nose against her neck.

She shivers. "Then do it."

It feels more like a challenge than anything else. If she thinks she can lay down a challenge like that in front of me and get away with it, then she's got another thing coming. I pull back and cock an eyebrow at her. "You serious?"

"Deadly," she replies, that playful grin playing at the corners of her mouth. "Tonight—I want you to—I want you to do something wild."

I eye her for a moment.

"I mean it." Looking at my lips, she slides her hand between us and grips my hard cock through my pants.

I can see the tipsiness in her eyes but I know this isn't because of the alcohol. We both want this. Maybe we both need it.

She tightens her grip slightly on my package.

That's all I need to push me over the edge. Oh, I'm going to make this girl scream.

I grab her, turn her around, and push her roughly down onto the bed. She lands with a slight giggle, scrambling to turn the right way up, but I shake my head, pulling off my blazer as I look down at her. "Stay like that," I order. "On your front. Don't look at me."

She raises her eyebrows and I can tell that she's swallowing down a smart remark, but she does as she's told, facing away from me, taking up on all fours so her ass is tilted towards me, wiggling back and forth temptingly.

"Wild?" I repeat softly, running my hand over the curve of her butt.

She shivers slightly. "Wild," she confirms, looking over her shoulder at me with a grin.

Without another word, I grab her dress and shove it roughly over her hips. Grabbing her panties, I yank them off of her with a sharp tearing sound of fabric. I toss them aside. She gasps when I grab her ankles and pull her towards me, running my hands up her legs until they come to rest on her ass.

"Show me your pussy," I order.

She obeys, as she tilts her hips forward and uses her fingers to open her folds for my viewing pleasure.

"Wider. I want to see it."

I look at her like this, her sweet little cunt opened up for me, and I admire the woman all laid out in front of me like this. Her delicious pussy is pink and glistening. A very tempting offer. My mouth starts to water, but I have other ideas for her tonight. I lean down and plant a soft kiss against her ass cheek then move over and press my tongue against her tight asshole.

She gasps again, and then lets out a long moan of pleasure as I move my tongue lightly back and forth across her butt, testing her. Her skin is sweet and clean and my cock is already rock-hard at the thought of pleasuring her like this. She slips a hand between her legs to play with her pussy, but I brush it away. "Not yet," I order, pulling back a little. "I'll tell you when you can touch yourself."

Sam groans in desperation but does as she's told, planting her hands in front of her.

I slide a hand over the small of her back to keep her in place and begin lapping at her tight hole, wondering if anyone has ever taken her here before. The thought of fucking her ass for the first time, of thoroughly devirginizing this gorgeous hole blows my mind, but for the time being I'm happy just to watch the way she reacts when I probe her with my tongue.

There's a specific pleasure in watching a woman driven so crazy with desire that she can't quite consummate yet and knowing you're the cause of it. And she doesn't let me down, groaning and wriggling while letting out these desperate little gasps as I trace my fingers up her thighs and towards her pussy without giving her any relief. She did say wild, and I'm going to show her just how delicious it is to offer someone like me that kind of deal.

Eventually, she gives in, murmuring the words that I've been longing to hear since the first moment I set eyes on her, "Fuck me, Lincoln," she pants the plea out.

I'm so into what I'm doing that I almost don't hear her the first time. I decide to continue, to really make her beg. "What was that?" I ask, pulling back and shooting a look at her.

Her face is painted with need, her jaw taut and her eyes bright. "Fuck me, please," she begs.

"Are you sure?" I ask innocently.

"Lincoln, I need this…"

"Need what?" I ask, stroking around the entrance to her pussy with one finger tauntingly.

She lets out a frustrated groan. "Need you inside me," she pleads. "Like this. Anyway you want. Please, just fuck me…"

I look down at her dripping pussy and know I can't hold back any longer. I have to have her. This is fun, but my cock is straining so hard against my pants, I fear I might do it damage.

"Don't move," I order as I pick up her shredded panties from the floor. Leaning forward, I prompt, "Open," as I tap her mouth. With her mouth open, I shove the panties between her lips, earning a surprised squeak as my reward. "We don't want Maddie to hear now, do we?" I murmur, stroking her chin and drawing her gaze to mine.

She nods and closes her eyes, wiggling her hips back and

forth, reminding me as if I need reminding that her pussy needs my cock inside it.

I pull down my pants. I'm so damn hard just by looking at the sight of her like this, desperate for me. Hell, it's almost enough to make me nut. I press myself to her entrance and her pussy instantly clenches around my cockhead. I look down at her, and grabbing her hips, sink my fingers into her flesh hard. "Fuck yourself on my cock," I order.

She turns her head and stares at me for a second before it sinks in.

I thrust an inch into her and then hold still, though it takes all my power to do so.

Sam seems to get the message, and begins to work herself back and forth on my dick. Spreading her cream on my cock, making it glisten.

I get to watch it all and the feeling is exquisite, but even better than the sensation of her hot, tight cunt desperately pushing itself up and down my dick is the sight of her doing this. She tips her head back and closes her eyes and even through the fabric of the panties, I can make out her deep, guttural groans of pleasure as she takes me in deep. I have never wanted anyone as badly as I want her in this moment, but I want to make her work for this. There's nothing better than seeing a woman so desperate for you that she'll do anything she can, to feel your cock inside of her.

Sam looks completely lost to pleasure.

I let her fuck me like that for a few more agonizing minutes, but having to hold back is killing me. My balls are tingling and my cock is aching for some real, deep fucking. Eventually, I can't take it anymore. I lean forward and grasp a handful of her hair in my hand. Then I begin to thrust into her. I go slow at first, matching her pace, but gradually the two of us are moving faster, harder, our bodies in perfect harmony.

A long, low muffled wail of pleasure emits from her mouth.

I feel a surge of triumph. I said I was going to make her scream and I did.

"You want to come?" I ask, leaning down and running my free hand up her spine.

She nods.

Oh no, I want to hear it. "I said, do you want to come?" I demand, pulling the panties out of her mouth.

"I need you to make me come," she almost growls at me, animalistic, a side of her I've never seen before.

I smile. *That's my girl.*

I gently stuff the panties back into her mouth and slide a hand down between her legs to stroke her clit, matching my movements with the pace of my thrusts, watching as her jaw clenches once more and her eyes roll back. She's moving as if on instinct now, her body taking over, every motion pushing her closer and closer.

I'm so focused on making her come that my own orgasm almost takes me by surprise. I tip my head back and let out a roar, forgetting Maddie is asleep in the next room. I bottom out inside of her. My cock twitches as I hold myself deep, making sure she can feel every pulsating inch of me as I empty my load in her.

She carries on, fucking me, her movements now frantic. Her body starts to arch and spasm. A moment later, I feel her come, her clit throbbing and her pussy clenching me as she milks the last of my climax from my erection.

Our bodies still, the two of us lost in this shared bubble of pleasure that takes a good long while to burst.

When it does, I slowly pull out of her, and slide down on the bed next to her.

Sam turns to me and I take the gag out of her mouth.

Leaning in, she plants a soft kiss on my lips. "I enjoyed that. Now I'm going to use my mouth to clean you up, you dirty, dirty boy you."

I laugh softly as she moves down along my body. Life is good.

EPILOGUE

SAMANTHA

One Year Later

"That sounds just great. We'll have the proposal over to you sometime in the next two or three days." I'm smiling when I hang up after talking to the representative of the company that will most likely be my next client. I fire off a quick email to my assistant, confirming she needs to get the finalized version of the proposal over to me for review.

"Sam?"

Maddie's knock at the door to my office is well-timed, and it's with a smile that I get up to answer. "What is it?" I ask, tussling her curly hair and taking her hand to let her lead me to the kitchen. One thing I love most about having my own consulting company is being able to work remotely. Why pay overhead for an office when I can do everything from home? I've been successful in the past year, but I'm nowhere near needing more space than what I have here.

Besides, there are situations in which working in my pajamas, with my feet up, might come in handy in the near future.

"I made lunch!" Maddie waves her arms with a flourish, showing off her handiwork. For a seven-year-old, she didn't do half bad. Tuna sandwiches, salad, and Nutella cookies.

"Very well done, young lady." I kiss the top of her head before shooing her into her chair. "Just make sure you finish all the good stuff before you start in on the *good* stuff."

She laughs impishly before I sit opposite her and we share lunch, and as we always do when she is on a school break. Sometimes, I can't believe my luck. I fell into the family I always wanted. She's such a great kid. Even after eight months of being married to her father, she hasn't lost her charm. I couldn't ask for a better stepdaughter.

"Are you finished working for the day?" she asks, chomping on a mouthful of sandwich.

"Yup. And Daddy should be home soon, too."

"Where is he? He doesn't work on Saturdays anymore."

"I know, and that's such a good thing. He had to pick something up from the store."

"Oh! Ice cream?"

"No!" I laugh. "Something even better. I promise." At least, I hope she thinks it's better. I know I do.

My husband gets home just after we've finished eating, and he's carrying a gift bag in one hand. My heart skips a beat, the way it always does when Lincoln enters the room. I never thought marriage could be like this. Lord knows, I didn't have the strongest example while I was growing up. Every day I get to wake up beside him is a joy, one which hasn't lost its magic over the past months.

"Ooh, what's that?" she asks, eyes wide. "Is it for me?"

"Maybe it's a gift for Sam. What do you think about that Big Eyes?" he teases, holding the bag high enough, so she can't reach it.

"No, it's not. It's for me. Sam told me," she says, hopping up and down with one arm outstretched.

Both Lincoln and I laugh. The kid doesn't miss a trick.

"Yes, it's for you," he says and hands over the bag.

I pat a spot beside me on the sofa, signaling for her to sit with me. My stomach's a little woozy, which is nothing new lately.

Our eyes meet over the top of her head as she fishes her gift out from the thick thatch of tissue paper. I can see he's just as nervous as I am. What if Maddie turns out to be one of those jealous kids who doesn't want to share the attention?

"What is this?" she asks.

"Open it, you big silly," Lincoln prompts.

She pulls out the t-shirt.

I hold my breath as she lets it unfold in front of her.

The words are clear. Big Sister.

We watch, neither of us saying a word, as she takes it all in silently.

"Honey?" I whisper, my throat is nearly choked with emotion.

"Sweetheart?" Lincoln asks, sliding an arm around her shoulders.

"Does this mean...I'm gonna get a brother or a sister?" She runs one hand across the front of the shirt over the words, as though she needs to touch it to believe the message.

"A brother," I explain. "You're going to have a baby brother. In around five months."

"Five months?" She jumps up, glaring at us. "I have to wait five whole months for the baby to come?"

"Um..." Lincoln and I exchange glances. "Does this mean you're happy?" he asks.

She stares at us curiously. "Why would I be anything else?"

"Um...Just us being silly," Lincoln replies.

She throws herself into his arms, squeezing him around the neck. "A baby! A brother! I'm gonna be a big sister?"

"You really are happy, honey?" I ask, my eyes misting. I couldn't bear it if Maddie had been moody or mad about the baby growing in my belly. It would have broken my heart.

She comes to me, smiling from ear to ear, and looks down at my belly. It's only ever-so-slightly swollen four months in. "Is he in your stomach now?" she whispers.

I nod, too choked up to speak.

"Do you want to see if you can feel him kick?" Lincoln asks.

Maddie frowns. "Is he being naughty? Is he kicking Sam?"

"No, honey, he is just moving around and that feels like a gentle prod."

"Ohhhh."

"So do you want to feel?"

She nods and places one palm over where the baby is sleeping. I've never seen such reverence in my life.

Lincoln takes my hand, his fingers closing over it, reminding me that I have everything.

Life is perfect.

SECOND EPILOGUE

LINCOLN

Five Months Later

"Come on over, sweetheart."

Maddie's eyes are as big dinner plates as I usher her to the bed where her stepmother and new baby brother are resting. It's been a long twenty-four hours, but definitely some of the happiest of my life.

Sam looks as though she feels much the same way, her eyes heavy with fatigue but a gentle smile firmly in place none-theless. She's exhausted, weak, her hair in a tangled bun, but she's never looked more beautiful or more overjoyed. All because she's holding her son in her arms.

Our son.

"Hi, honey," Sam coos when she sees Maddie with me. "I'm so glad you're here. This little man has been anxious to meet his big sister."

Maddie seems to almost swell up with pride at the thought of being the new baby's big sister. "He has?" she asks in a hushed whisper. "I wanted to meet him, too." She walks over to the side of the bed.

I lift her up and put her on the bed so she can sit beside Sam and the baby. Jacob. My boy.

"He's so small," she whispers in awe.

"He is small," Sam replies, stroking Maddie's hair. "But I'm pretty sure he recognizes your voice by now, too. I'm sure of it. From all those books, you read to him. You should talk to him."

"I should? His eyes are closed so he must be sleeping. I thought you weren't supposed to wake babies up when they're sleeping."

Sam and I laugh gently at this.

Sam smiles at her. "Sure, but I don't think you'll wake him right now. He's had a very, very long first day of life. But he does want to be with you. Do you think you want to hold him for a little while?"

My daughter gasps softly, like her stepmother just voiced a dream she didn't dare speak aloud. "Can I? I would love it."

"Of course." Sam shows her how to hold her arms and very carefully puts the bundle half in her hand and half in her lap.

I'm fairly sure my heart will explode with love as I watch my wife hand our son to our daughter. It's the most precious moment of my life.

Maddie looks down into the baby's face, examining him closely. She looks up at me, then at Sam, and starts bawling— like ugly crying.

"Sweetheart, what is it?" I ask, moving to her side to hold her close to me. I don't want her to feel like she's second best now, like she doesn't count anymore. She's my first. And no child no matter how many come will ever take her place.

It isn't that at all. "I'm just so happy," she weeps, leaning against my chest, still holding her baby brother. "I'm so happy."

I look to Sam, whose eyes are also sparkling with unshed tears, just like mine are. Yes. I know how Maddie feels.

The End

THE PROMISE

COMING SOON...

Georgia Le Carre

&

River Laurent

COLE

Her smell is in my nostrils, which is plum stupid because while it's true she is back in town, but she's miles away. Letty, who runs the Lake hotel called to tell that she arrived last night. From that moment on, I stopped being able to function. Damnit to hell all I want to do is hold her again.

My body feels like it is a tiny iron filling and there is a giant magnet pulling at it. The draw is so strong I have to clench my hands into fists to stop myself from grabbing my car keys and going to her. *She fuckin' hates you. Let it alone. You've survived all these years. Just damn well leave it alone, Cole Finley.*

I glance at my watch for the hundredth time and pace the floor of my library restlessly. The funeral must surely be over by now.

A car comes up the driveway, and I stride over to the window. Impatiently, I watch my mother take her time getting out of her car and walk up to the door. She is still dressed in the black outfit she wore to the funeral. I turn away from the window, relax my hands, and wait while she travels through my house, and stands at the doorway.

"What does she look like?" My voice is hoarse and throbbing with need.

My mother's eyes widen with surprise. Then, with a defeated sigh, she heads to the drinks cabinet. Barely able to control myself, I wait while she pours out a large measure of vodka. No chaser. She drinks it down as if she needs it and slams the glass down on the counter. "She looks like a star," she says flatly.

I run my hands through my hair. "But does she look happy?"

My mother raises her eyebrows. "She was attending her step-mother's funeral after all so one shouldn't really expect cartwheels."

I stare at her with frustration, my shoulders tense. "You know what I mean. Does she look like she is happy with her life? Like she made the right decision to leave here?"

My mother shrugs delicately and walks over to a sofa. She settles herself and leans back on the leather. "It's hard to say, but she looks like she no longer belongs in Black Rock."

My chest tightens with pain. Even breathing hurts. "Was she there…alone?"

My mother's eyes fill with pity. "Yes."

That one word feels like fireworks exploding inside my body. "Ma."

"Yes?"

"I need to see her again."

My mother's face tightens. "Don't do that, Cole. She'll be gone by tomorrow and your life will go back to what it was. Don't spoil it. Don't make it harder for yourself...and her."

"I just want to see her for a moment."

My mother leans forward. Dr. Westwood's injections have made it impossible for her to frown, but I know that expression. She is trying to. "It's a terrible idea Cole."

"I don't fucking care."

"Oh, darling. She'll destroy you."

I start backing away from her. "I just want to see how she is. After all this time, no one can't begrudge me that one thing. If she's truly happy, I'll walk away. I swear it."

"Cole," my mother calls, but I am already gone.

I get into my car and hit the accelerator hard. The wheels spin on the asphalt. All those years ago she broke me, and maybe she will again, but I don't care. I have to see her one more time. There's been no one since she left. Every woman leaves me cold. No matter what they do or say it is no good. My cock is numb.

It is waiting for only one woman. Her.

TAYLOR

A light spring breeze lifts the side-swept bangs off my forehead. The air smells clean with a hint of freshly dug earth. It makes a heavenly change from the smog of LA. I breathe it deeply into my lungs. Through the lenses of my dark glasses, I watch the priest say the last rites. His voice is gravelly and solemn.

"Ashes to ashes, dust to dust."

There should be sadness in my heart. Instead there is nothing. I think of her as she was. Beautiful and cold. No, cold is the wrong word. I guess she was bitter. She always viewed me as the competition, but when Dad died and left the house to me with the provision that she could live her life out in it, I became the enemy. How she hated me, silently, coldly, viciously.

While I lived with her I hated her back with an equal intensity, but after I left with a broken heart, I understood her bitterness. My father shouldn't have left the house to me. It was a betrayal. He should have left it to her. She was his wife.

I sent her money every month even though she neither acknowledged it, or thanked me.

I look down at my black Louboutins. I should have known better than to wear them. The heels are too high, and if don't hold them with the spikes hovering slightly above the ground, they sink into the soft earth.

The priest stops speaking and turns his head to look at me.

I drop the red rose in my hand on the white casket and I turn around to leave. People I have not seen or heard for ten years mill around me. They wear concerned expressions, well-meaning faces filled with genuine kindness and regret. They are good people. I grew up with them. Almost family. But I can't let them unravel me.

Smiling vaguely at no one in particular I quickly start walking towards my car. Marco, my driver rushes to open the door of the hired car. I slip in smoothly. He closes the door and I exhale. I've done my duty. I've given her a good burial.

Marco gets in and winds the partition down. "Hotel?"

"Yes," I confirm quietly.

"Right," He nods and actives the remote partition upwards.

"Wait," I blurt out. "No. Not the hotel. Take me to my mother's house first."

"Got it," he says smartly.

The car goes through the streets. It is like being in a time warp.

Nothing has changed, Dairy Queen, Tucker's Diner, the

plastic dog outside the hardware shop. There's old Jenkins sitting outside his tattoo shop sunning himself with a beer can in his hand. His face is pure leather, but he is still alive and well. We used to pop firecrackers into his mailbox and he would run out of his house his face purple with rage, screaming blue murder.

Marco drives up to the house.

The shutters are drawn. There is a sad air of stillness and neglect around it.

"You can go back to the hotel, Marco. I'll call you in the morning."

"You're sure?"

I nod and get out of the car. It is strange not be mobbed by paparazzi and fans. Actually, it's rather wonderful not to have to run like a criminal from the car to the door all the time. For years, I believed I wanted fame. I wanted to be recognized everywhere I went. I wanted to be a big star, but now I know I don't.

Marco drives away and I go up the wooden steps to the wide porch. I glance at the rocking chair at one corner and feel an odd twinge. A feeling. How strange. I haven't felt anything for years. My cell rings, the sound muted, but oddly jarring. As if my other busy life has already come to intrude. I take it out of my purse and look at the screen. It's Nick, my manager. I walk to the rocking chair. Sitting in it I click accept.

"Where are you now?" he asks.

"At the house."

"You mean the funeral is already over?"

"Yeah," I reply distantly. I don't want to talk to him. The sound of the chair creaking against the wood is soothing. My mother used to sit here a lot with me in her lap after she fell ill. I close my eyes. Memories swarm back. Memories of Mom, memories of Dad, memories of Cole. My stomach clenches into a painful knot. I push the images away and open my eyes.

"Are you all right?" Nick sounds concerned, whether for me or my career is hard to tell, but he is definitely genuinely concerned.

"Yes." My voice is clipped and hard.

"You sure you don't want me to come?"

"Absolutely. I'm not hanging around long, anyway. I'll be leaving tomorrow afternoon."

"That's good. There's nothing left for you in that godforsaken town."

"No," I agree, but an ache deep inside me starts to throb. I left something here, Nick. I left my heart.

"All right, then. Call me if you need anything, or if you just want to talk, okay?"

"Okay."

"Love you," he says.

"Call you later."

I end the call, close my eyes and try to think of Nick's warm brown eyes. He cares about me. I have a good life in LA.

My eyes are drawn to the magnolia tree. The swing is gone, but the treehouse is still there. I bite my lip. Maybe later I will go and explore it. I slip my shoes off, take the key from under the flower pot, and open the front door. Inside it is dim and full of still shadows.

I close the door and lean against it. I breathe in the stale and musty. Underneath it there is a strong chemical odor of medicine. My step-mother lived here alone for the last six years.

For a moment, I have an overwhelming desire to walk out of the house, and call Marco to come back and take me to the hotel, then I decide that I don't want to see anyone at the hotel. I'm tired and I just want to sleep.

The doorbell rings and the sound startles me. I look through the peephole and see Mrs. Tucker from next door standing outside. She is in her Sunday best. Suppressing a sigh, I open the door.

"Hello Taylor. I've brought you some casserole. I thought maybe we could have lunch together."

I hang on to the doorknob and plaster a smile on my face. "Thank you, Mrs. Tucker. That is so kind of you, but honestly, I'm just not in the mood to eat anything right now."

Her face fall which kinda makes me feel guilty, but I just can't face having to make small talk with anyone right now. She holds the container out to me. "Well then, honey, you eat it when you feel like it. I'll be at home if you need me."

Reluctantly, I take the casserole that I know I will never eat. "Thank you."

She turns to go then spins back. "I've followed your career, you know. You've done our little town proud, my girl. Both Mr. Tucker and I are very proud of you."

"Thank you, Mrs. Tucker."

"Well, I just though you should know."

"It's very kind of you to say that. Thank you." I smile again.

"Well, all right. I'll be going, then."

"Good bye, Mrs. Tucker."

I put the casserole on the kitchen table and the doorbell goes again. With a frown, I go to answer it. It'll probably be another neighbor bearing more food I can't eat. I don't even bother to look through the peephole this time. I open the door and smile at Betty Crankshaw. She is wearing a blue hat and carrying a cake tin.

"I've brought some muffins for you, love. I know you love blueberry muffins."

COLE

I rush through a red traffic light and turn into Mullholland drive. God, I've not been here ever since she left. I park the car outside her mother's house. I walk up to the door and ring the bell. It goes unanswered for a long time and I'm about to ring it again when she opens the door.

The moment I see her face I regret ever letting her go. My heart aches with need. God, how stupid I was. What a fucking kid I must have been to have let her go.

And for what?

Look at her.

She's not happy.

She used to glow with happiness. I should have chained her to me instead of letting her go to carve her name in lights. It was a mistake. I have to make her fall back in love with me again.

Her full lips part. "Cole," she breathes and for a second it is as if no time has passed. The other kids are singing Cole and Casey K-i-s-s-i-n-g in the Tree to us. She's my girl and I've come around to take her to the movies. I stare at her mouth. I'm dying for a taste. She used to taste like honey.

Then the past disappears like smoke, and her eyes become hard. "What do you want, Finlay?"

"You," I say.

Something flashes in her eyes. "You're a bastard, you know."

"I shouldn't have let you go, Taylor."

"Get out of my house," she growls.

"I'm not leaving without you."

"What? she sneers. "Did you fall somewhere and hit your little head? Because we were finished ten years ago."

"We're not finished until I say so."

She moves suddenly to slam the door and I put my palm on it completely arresting its movement.

"Do I need to call the police?" she huffs, her eyes stormy.

"All I want to do is talk to you."

"There's nothing to talk about." Her voice is bitter.

"Then it'll be a very short conversation, won't it?"

She sighs and moves away from the door. "Say what you need to say and get out."

I go into the house and close the door. She leads the way into her mother's sitting room.

'Talk," she says, folding her arms in front of her body.

I walk up to her. "Did you achieve everything you wanted to? Was it worth it?"

"Yes," she snarls, her voice trembling defiantly. "I grabbed the opportunity when it presented itself and I left this godforsaken town."

I stare down at her glittering eyes. "No regrets?"

"None." The word is clipped like a bullet.

I look at her face and feel as if I cannot go another minute without making her mine. "Well, I have. I should have done it differently. I want you, Taylor. I've been wanting you for the last ten years. I've waited all this time, but no more. I won't be denied for another second. I'm going to have you right now."

Her eyes widen. "No," she gasps, but I notice she doesn't move away. I wrap my hands around her too thin body, and my mouth descends down on hers, crushing, hungry, fierce.

She whimpers with the force of my kiss.

I lean in and lift her up into my arms. Her hands go around my neck. Her round eyes stare up at me, helpless, vulnerable…mine. I lift her into my arms. Fuck, it's like picking up a child. Doesn't she ever eat anything in LA?

I carry her up the stairs. She burrows her face in my chest, but I can feel her trembling in my arms. I kick the door open to her old room. Her stepmother has kept it almost exactly how it was when she was living there.

I lay her on the single bed and look down at her.

She is about to find out that she belongs to me and only me.

To be continued…

AFTERWORD

Thank you for reading!
For the latest news please click on the link below to receive info about my latest releases and giveaways.

CAN WE TALK?

and remember

Or come and say hello here:

FACEBOOK